EXTRA BROWN SUGAR, PLEASE

KEISHA ELLE

TEXT UCP TO 22828 TO SUBSCRIBE TO OUR MAILING LIST
If you would like to join our team, submit the first 3-4 chapters of
your completed manuscript to
Submissions@UrbanChaptersPublications.com

To John...My firstborn, we grew up together. Although I was too young to be raising a child, the choices I made had me doing just that. Our journey may have started off rough, but together -we got through it! Remember...if no one else has your back, I always will. I love you with everything in me!

1

FEBRUARY 10TH

SHUGG

"I love you, Mrs. Bonner," Cedric whispered in my ear. I smiled as he began to trace soft kisses down the side of my face.

"I love you too, Mr. Bonner, but you're getting ahead of yourself, aren't you? We're not married yet."

"We should be," Cedric continued, letting his arms roam freely down my naked body. "It's your fault. You should have kept my son cooking a few more days."

Our son, Cree, was seven months old and had terrible timing. Not only did he exit the confines of my body two months early, he made his entrance on the morning I was scheduled to walk down the aisle.

"It's not my fault," I huffed. "He's stubborn, just like his daddy."

"You love me though." His strong hands pushed me onto my back. "Stubborn or not, you know you can't live without me."

He was right. I loved my man. We had been through hell and high back and finally, we were together. We started out as friends. Years later, we became lovers. Now, we were inseparable.

"Whatever! You're the one who can't live without me."

I inhaled deeply as he positioned himself on top of me. His lips pressed up against mine as his body inched downward. He kissed my chin, my collarbone, and between my breasts. He continued on, kissing over my round stomach. My son wasn't even one yet, and I was five-months pregnant again.

"Do you hear your momma talking crazy to me?" he spoke to my belly. "She knows how much I love her ass. Of course, I can't live without her."

I blushed. Cedric was so sweet; almost to the point of being too good to be true. I was the luckiest woman in the world; except at that moment. Cree decided to test how strong his lungs were. His cry activated his feeding machine, and my breasts instantly became fuller and started leaking. 'Adult time' was over before it started.

"I'll get him," Cedric grunted, rolling off me. His dick stood at attention as he walked naked out of the room.

I was beyond frustrated. My pregnancy had my hormones all over the place and I needed some sex! It was like my son could sense intimacy was about to take place. Every time Cedric and I were about to get it in, Cree somehow found a way to interfere. Unfortunately for us, our dedicated babysitter thought a two-week vacation in Mexico was more important than spending time with her grandson. Cedric's mother, Mary, hadn't so much as picked up the phone to check on Cree since she left. All I needed was a good hour for Cedric to beat it up, and I would be good. Was that too much to ask?

I could have easily called my best friend, Davina. If I needed her, she would drop everything just to help me out. The only problem was, I felt guilty. She spent so much time in Florida with both her Miami law firm and her husband's club, that when she came back home, she just wanted to chill. I didn't want to deprive her of that. She worked hard. She deserved some time to relax. My horniness would just have to wait.

I sat up in the bed, as Cedric strolled in with Cree smiling in his arms. When he saw me, he damn he tried his best to break free. I was his milk supply. He couldn't get to me fast enough. Cedric extended him in my direction, and I grabbed him. He immediately latched on to one of my bare breasts.

"Damn, Cree!" I hollered. His two bottom teeth roughly scraped against my nipple. "That shit hurt! Your ass is about to go on the damn bottle!"

"Thank God!" Cedric interjected. "Maybe I'll get my titties back."

I shook my head as my phone began to ring on the nightstand. I leaned over and examined the name before picking it up. It was Davina. I moved Cree to my other breast and answered her call.

"What's up, girl?"

"Nothing much. Just seeing if you're almost ready?"

"No. Shit, what time is it?" I removed the phone from my ear and examined the time.

"Almost five. It's still early, I know, but we both know how long it takes you to get ready."

"Perfection takes time," I said in my own defense. "I'm a walking billboard for myself. If I look like shit when I step outside, why would anyone trust me enough to get them together? I'm a business. A brand. A-"

"Okay, okay. Save me the dramatics. You just ain't ready. Well, I'll be leaving out of here within the hour. Do you want me to swing by and get you, or are you driving yourself?"

"I'll drive myself. I don't want to hold you up. I'm feeding Cree, and then I have to shower and get ready. I don't know what time I'm gonna be out."

"I'm warning you now...you know how Nessa is. She's on time with everything. If she says dinner is served at 7PM, dinner is served at 7PM. If you ain't there, you get skipped. I got a peek at the menu. It's worth being on time."

"I'll try my best," I advised.

"Oh, and by the way, tell Cedric to make sure Cree has his bag. Chandra was just gonna watch him for the bachelor party, but it'll probably end late. He might as well stay the night."

"I'll let him know," I advised as I glanced over at Cedric. He was so engrossed in his own phone, that he wasn't paying me the least bit of attention. "I'll see you at Nessa's house."

After Davina snuck off and married her boyfriend, Genesis, her in-laws practically became mine. I was like Davina's sister, which made her family, my family. Her mother-in-law, Chandra, was the mother I wish I had. She was cool as hell, but brutally honest.

The guys were cool, but it's the women that I developed a closeness with. Nessa was married to Genesis' brother, Steele. She was slowly becoming one of my good friends. Genesis' sister, Bliss was cool too, but we didn't click like Nessa and I did. Genesis' brother Emory had a whole sleuth of women, but up until recently, he was holding it down with Stephanie. The two of us didn't get along over some stupid shit. I tried to keep it classy, but the chick just didn't like me. We said 'hi' and 'bye' when we saw each other, but that's about it.

Cree fell asleep in my arms. His heavy butt didn't want to do anything but eat and sleep. Easing off the bed, I passed him to Cedric on my way to the bathroom. Cedric laid him on his stomach in our bed and leaned forward to smack my ass. Cree's head popped up like a meerkat searching for a predator.

"Hater," Cedric smirked. "You can lay on back down, lil nigga, I ain't gettin' none."

As if on cue, Cree lowered his head and closed his eyes. Within seconds, he was snoring softly.

"Do you have any plans tonight?" I asked over my shoulder.

"Genesis and Ty are coming over. We're gonna catch the Cavs' game and have a few beers."

"Really? That's weird. Chandra seems to think she's watching Cree tonight. She said make sure you have his bag ready. Is there anything you need to tell me?"

"Look, baby, I was dragged into this."

"Dragged into a bachelor party? Really, Cedric. You couldn't think of a better lie than that?" I entered the bathroom and peered at myself in the mirror. I had a lot of work to do.

"It's not a lie. It's the truth."

"Cedric...it's okay," I reassured him, peeking my head out the bathroom. "It's cool. Enjoy yourself. Have fun with the fellas. I'll be with the girls. Just remember...you have a woman at home that's horny as fuck, and our son won't be back until the morning."

"Text me when you're on your way home. I'll meet you here."

I smiled as I started the shower. My man wanted me just as bad as I wanted him.

DAVINA

"No, you didn't!" I fussed. "Genesis! Why didn't you pull out?"

"I'm sorry, baby. It was just feelin' so good."

I pushed my husband back and sat up in the bed. "Bullshit. I told you I ain't tryin' to have no kids."

"It was an accident."

"Accident, my ass." I stood up and stomped toward the bathroom. Genesis was right on my heels.

"Davina, don't be like that."

"Genesis, we talked about this. We said we would be married at least five years before we started having kids. We've only been married a year."

"And it's been the best year of my life." I reached for the knob to turn on the shower, but he stopped me. "I know what you said. But, that's what *you* want. I want you to have my baby."

"I will. In four years."

"No, now. I want a couple shorties runnin' around."

"You're crazy."

I turned the water on and eased around him. I was tired of explaining myself. I loved my husband with all my heart, but I wasn't in a rush to have kids. I had two law firms, in two different cities, both doing exceptionally well. There was also Genesis' gentleman's club that I helped manage. I barely had enough time for myself. All my spare time was spent overdoing the wifely duties I had neglected. I didn't have the time, nor patience needed to raise a child. Besides, I was scared.

"I ain't crazy, Davina. I just don't understand. What's the big deal anyway? I ain't going nowhere and I damn sure ain't lettin' you get away. So, what's the problem? If you have a baby in four years, you're still having *my* baby. Why put it off? Why can't we have a baby now?"

"What's the rush?"

He looked at me and shook his head. "You're right. Ain't no rush. It is what it is."

He walked off, leaving me standing there alone. My husband had baby fever, and it was my own fault. I had my nephew, Cree, rotten. It was so bad that he had a room in our house. I even took him to Miami with me a few times. Cree was my baby. Then, he became Genesis' baby. My husband started spending more time with Cree than I did. He had the boy down in the strip club, while he tended to his business. I don't know how many hoes poor Cree endured before I got there. Genesis worked almost as much as I did. Neither of us had the time to devote to a child.

"Genesis! Come back here!"

He appeared in the doorway and sighed heavily. "What?"

"Don't be like that. I'ma give you a baby. I just want to have you to myself for a while." I walked over to him to emphasize my point. I wrapped my arms around his toned midsection and rested my head on his chest. "Is that so bad?"

"Yes, it is. I want a baby, and you're gonna give me one."

He pulled me into the bathroom and into the shower. The water was warm and felt good against my skin. It felt almost as good as Genesis' hands maneuvering their way between my legs.

"What do you think you're doing?" I asked as I bit down on my bottom lip. I knew exactly what he was doing. He was getting me ready for round number two.

"I'm about to get what I want," he said as he slowly entered me. "You want me to stop?"

I didn't say a word. I couldn't speak. It felt so damn good. My body was in a state of tranquil bliss. I didn't want him to stop. He turned me around, pushed me back into the shower wall, lifted a leg, and entered me again. The hair that I was trying not to get wet was drenched. Genesis didn't care, he continued on, steadily increasing his speed.

"Do you love me?" he asked.

"Of course, I do," I responded breathily.

"Well, let me give you a baby."

"Gen-"

"Please," he continued, cutting me off. Something about the way he said it did something to me. It was sexy and had me losing the good sense God gave me.

"Okay."

That's all he needed to hear. Seconds later, he was moaning softly and busting deep inside me.

"That's what I'm talking about. I know you're pregnant now," he gloated. He carefully slid out of me and resumed his shower.

"Boy, that was only one time."

"Twice," he corrected.

"My bad, twice. It takes years for some people. Two times ain't really gonna make a difference."

"Shiiit. I got that super sperm. My shit goes straight to the target." He looked at my stomach as if he could see through me. "It's happening right now. My lil' nigga just got through. We're having a boy."

"You play too much."

He stepped out and wrapped a towel around his waist. "I ain't playin'. Just wait until it's time for your period. Don't act surprised when I tell you, 'I told you so.'"

I let that fool have his moment. He was all giddy and shit like he really did something.

Genesis was dressed by the time I made my way into the room. I quickly slid into my long-sleeved sheath dress. It was the only thing I had that was all white. I could have bought something new, but it was just us girls. It wasn't that serious.

"Damn," he mouthed, watching me apply my makeup. "You sure you wanna go? We can always stay home and, you know." His wink confirmed that he wanted a repeat of what we had already done *twice*.

"Do I wanna go and am I going are two different things. I already promised Nessa."

"Promises can be broken."

He slowly crept behind me. I continued applying my makeup as if he wasn't even there. It was hard not to notice him though. Genesis was tall, fit, and fine.

"Come on, Davina. Stay here. We can get back in the bed."

"I know you ain't gonna miss Steele's bachelor's party. Don't you wanna see the half-naked girls shaking their ass in front of you?"

"I see pussy all day every day. If it ain't yours, I ain't impressed."

"Remember that when they're all up on you."

I picked up my phone as it rung beside me. I thought it was going to be Shugg asking where I was. I scolded her about being on time, and I was running late myself. Instead of Shugg's number showing up on the phone's caller ID, the number for my office appeared.

"Hey, Sharon," I answered as cheerfully as I could. "It's late. Is everything okay?"

"Yes, Mrs. St. John. Everything's fine."

She knew I hated the formalities. I considered my staff family. She didn't have to be so proper all the time.

"Davina," I corrected.

"I'm sorry, Davina. I just wanted to tell you about a request that came through. A woman is seeking representation for her divorce. I thought you might be interested."

"I'm swamped. I told you I'm not taking on any more cases right now. My Miami load is enough for both locations."

"I know, but this one is different. Stanley Weeks is representing the woman's husband."

"Stanley?" I raised a perfectly arched eyebrow at my arch nemesis' name. "It's good to see he's working again. I thought he fell off the face of the earth."

"He's back alright...and they're already trying to play hardball. You should see their list of demands."

"Put her on my calendar for some time next week," I advised. "I'll be in touch."

"What are you smiling for?" Genesis asked as I hung up the phone.

"Looks like I might be facing off against Stanley again in court. I've been waiting for months to see him again. That's the best news I've heard all day."

Genesis kissed me on the cheek and grabbed his car keys. "The good news just keeps coming."

"You had good news today, too?" I questioned.

"Sure did. I found out I was gonna be a daddy."

I choked on my own saliva. I set myself up for that one. "Stop playing, Genesis!"

"Who's playing? You're about to have my baby, girl. Just wait and see."

BLISS

"You better not be entertaining those sluts," I warned my boyfriend, Ty. "Believe me; I'll find out if you do."

The permanent smile etched on his face as he got dressed for my brother's bachelor party had me thinking twice about going to Nessa's dinner. I had trust issues. Although Ty had never done anything to warrant my feelings, I was still skeptical. He was naïve and a sucker for a pretty face.

"Why would I be doing that?" Ty stopped brushing the deep waves on top of his head and turned to me. His dark, handsome face stared at me curiously. "You gotta stop doing this. We've been together since high school, Bliss. We're grown now. If I wanted to do something, I would have done it already."

He continued brushing the hair I convinced him to cut. For two years, he grew dreads. Once they became a decent length, his female fan base grew significantly. Suddenly, everyone with a pussy wanted to play in my man's hair and tell him how handsome he looked. It wasn't really everybody, but that's how I felt. I put my foot down and made him cut that shit off.

"So, you thought about it?" I quizzed, twisting his words.

"No, Bliss. *Damn.* I got what I need. You and my son are the most important people in my life. I'm happy with you and only you. Now chill the hell out!"

I couldn't 'chill out.' I had to protect my investment. Ty didn't have shit but a decent stroke when I got with him, and even that came a long way. He was putting it down in the bedroom, and there was no way in hell I was gonna give another female the opportunity to sample what was mine.

"Fuck it. I'll just roll with you. I'm sure Nessa will understand."

I dialed my sister-in-law's number as Ty began to mumble under his breath. He knew how I was. When I felt threatened, I turned into a different person.

"Hey, Nessa," I began when she answered the phone. "I know it's short notice but..."

The joke was on me. Nessa flipped that shit around and had me agreeing to make last minute stops at her crib.

"Bliss, I'm so glad you called. Can you stop by my house and get my pearl necklace? I can't believe I forgot it."

"A pearl necklace? Nessa, that's all the way across town! Why don't you ask Steele to bring it to you?"

"I tried, but he's not answering the phone. Please, sis. The photographer will be here at eight, and I need my necklace. I can't take pictures with a bare neck."

"Why can't you?" I huffed.

"Because, I can't. Thanks, Bliss. You're the best! I owe you."

"Wait...Nessa..."

She hung up before I could tell her I wasn't coming. I grunted in frustration.

"What's all that for?" Ty asked.

"Nessa got me running errands for her ass. Look at me. Do I look like I should be driving around town for a damn necklace?"

Ty studied me and nodded in appreciation. I know Nessa wanted everyone to be formal, but I found the cutest white strapless jumpsuit, and I was putting it to use. I paired it with a peep toe stiletto heel, and a white feathered fascinator hat.

"You look like you're ready for something else," Ty teased, extending his arms toward me.

I stepped back quickly. "Boy! I'm wearing white! You know I can't be getting dirty."

"I can't help myself." Ty stepped toward me again and I swatted his hands away.

"I'll help you out. I'm leaving." I slid my arms into my favorite coat, made of thick rabbit fur. It was white and accented my look.

"I thought you were rolling with me."

"I might pop up when you least expect it. Right now, I gotta go get this damn necklace for Nessa." I started toward the door but stopped just before opening it. "I got eyes in the back of my head. Remember that. I see everything, and what I don't, my brothers will tell me."

"You got issues, Bliss. I love you, though. I'll take our son to your mom and then I'll be on my way. You want the address to where I'll be?" he offered with a smirk. "You know, just in case you want to pop up."

"No need. I'll just trace your phone when I'm ready." I blew him an air kiss and slammed the door behind me.

I drove twenty-five minutes out of my way to get to Nessa and Steele's house. Seeing Steele's car in the driveway had me fuming. He could have answered his wife's call and saved me the unnecessary drive time. I was gonna give it to my big brother when I saw him. I didn't bother knocking on the door. The knob turned without resistance and I simply walked in.

I opened my mouth to yell my brother's name, but voices echoing in the distance stopped me. I couldn't make out the words, but I definitely recognized Steele's voice. The other voice was soft, quiet, and female. What the fuck was my brother doing?

Following the sound, I ascended the stairs. The voices became crystal clear as a conversation I didn't want to hear played out in front of me.

"I'm pregnant, Steele."

"And? How do you know it's mine?"

"Because it is. You're the only one I've been with."

"Yeah, that's what you say. That could be anybody's baby. Don't try to blame that shit on me."

"I swear to you," she pleaded. "It's yours."

He sighed loudly before softening his tone. "A'ight. What are you gonna do about it?"

I had heard enough. I stepped through the partially opened door and let my presence be known. "What the fuck is going on here?"

The girl gasped loudly, but Steele was as cool as can be.

"What's up, sis?" he questioned nonchalantly. He walked over to me and kissed me on the cheek. "You look nice."

"Uh, Steele, can I talk to you for a minute?"

Steele followed me out the room, leaving his guest standing there. I refused to talk in front of her. I wasn't sure how much she already knew.

"What's up?" Steele asked me again. "Is everything okay?"

"No, it's not. Your *wife* sent me here to get her necklace because *you* weren't answering the damn phone. I get here, and this is the shit I walk into? What the fuck were you thinking, Steele? You got that bitch pregnant? You're about to renew your vows in four fuckin' days!"

"It's all good, baby sis. Let me worry about that. What necklace did she want?"

I followed Steele back to his bedroom. He retrieved Nessa's jewelry box and allowed me to roam through it freely. I grabbed the only pair of pearls and handed the box back to Steele.

"Do you have something I can put it in?" I quizzed.

"Yeah, hold on."

He disappeared into his walk-in closet. I took the opportunity to look over the chick who couldn't seem to keep her eyes off me. She was pretty; I'll give her that. She was dark-skinned with big almond eyes, a button nose, and full lips. Her hair was twisted up into a messy bun. She had the same shape that all the hoes Steele fucked with had; big titties, small waist, wide hips, and a round ass. She offered a shy smile, and I broke the gaze. I felt awkward as hell.

"You must be, Bliss," she mentioned, catching me off guard.

"How do you know my name?"

"Steele talks about you a lot. It's nice to finally meet you. I'm Chrysette." She extended her hand in my direction, and I just looked at it.

"That's nice." I stepped closer to the closet to see if Steele was coming. He was rummaging through some shit and sighing heavily. I took the opportunity to grill the chick. "How old are you?"

"Nineteen."

Young and dumb, I thought to myself. "So, you're pregnant?"

"Yeah," she said just above a whisper. "I just found out. I can't believe it."

"And you think it's my brother's? Are you sure?"

"Positive. Just like I was with the first one."

"First one? Wait? What? What do you mean first one?"

My face scrunched in confusion as Steele emerged with a white jewelry gift box in his hand. "Here you go, Bliss. This should do."

"Steele, what the hell is going on?" I took the box and crossed my arms over my chest. "This isn't the first time you got this girl pregnant?"

"You haven't told her?" I could see the pain in Chrysette's eyes as she questioned my brother.

For the first time since my arrival, Steele was at a loss for words. I looked back and forth between the two of them. Someone needed to tell me something.

"Tell me what? What the hell is going on?"

Steele took a deep breath. "It ain't the first time." He ran his hands over his short fade and sighed. "I got a daughter."

All the color drained from my face. Why didn't I keep my ass at home?

STEPHANIE

Part of me didn't want to go to Nessa's dinner. Emory and I had only been dating for a couple months, and I didn't feel that my presence was warranted. I mean, I wasn't *really* part of the family. I didn't even consider myself a close friend just yet, but I promised my man that I would go. I wanted him to know that I was making a conscious effort to get to know his family. So, that meant a lot of fake laughs and painted on smiles.

The girls weren't really that bad. Bliss was cool. She was loud and talked a lot, but she had a heart of gold. Whenever I needed to vent, or just needed someone to talk to, she would drive all the way to my crib, just be a listening ear. I couldn't tell you the number of times she answered my late-night calls. She didn't judge me for having a child, or that I was six years older than her brother. When her own mother gave me the third degree about my age, Bliss came to my rescue. I appreciated her much more than she knew.

Nessa was okay. I really didn't know her that well. She was too busy following behind Steele. She kept that man on a tight leash, and I wondered how in the hell they managed to stay married for as long as they did. In a few days, they would be celebrating their fifth wedding anniversary. The day was being honored with a vow renewal ceremony. The guys were living it up, throwing Steele a 'second' bachelor's party. Nessa chose to keep it boring and have a girl's dinner. Why couldn't we see some toned bodies and dicks swinging? She did weird shit like that.

There's a chick named Ashley that Reno brings over every now-and-then, but I've only seen her a handful of times. She's young, so she doesn't really count. Reno too. He's the baby of the family and rarely comes around.

Then there's Davina. Out of everybody, she's the most down-to-earth. That girl is smart as hell and can recite the law like it's nobody's business. I heard she's a lawyer, but she doesn't talk about it much. If her friend Shugg is around, she doesn't say much of anything. I'm sure Shugg filled her in on all our drama. You see, Shugg had sex with my now ex-husband, Jett, while we were married. She *claims* didn't know he was married, but that's beside the point. It's weird being around another woman who has been with your man. Well, ex-man. I'll be honest; it's weird as hell. I get an awkward feeling every time she's around. I know tonight will be no different. Nessa not only invited Davina; she invited her sidekick Shugg too.

I pulled up in front of Ramona's house and honked the horn. After our divorce, Jett moved in with his mother, so he watched our daughter there. Ari was having an overnight visit with her father, while I kicked it at Nessa's dinner.

"Where are you going looking like that?" Jett asked as I stepped out the car.

I rolled my eyes and opened my daughter's door. "None of your business."

Jett had some nerve questioning me about my whereabouts. During our marriage, he stepped out on me more than a few times. Shugg was one of his snacks on the side, along with her man's former wife, Tranique. The love triangle is crazy, I know!

"You're my daughter's mother. It's always gonna be my business." He stepped into my personal space. "Just like you're always gonna be my business. I'm gonna always love you, Stephanie. Just like you're gonna always love me."

I peered at the man I once loved. He was too handsome for his own good. His smooth caramel skin, and dark, loose curls that had me in love before I graduated high school. Against my parent's request, I married him and brought him into my lifestyle. My family had money, and when Jett became my husband, so did he. It went straight to his head. When his indiscretions came to light, I left and didn't look back.

"The love is long gone. You're Ari's father. It's not about you. It's not about me. It's about this little girl." I pointed to our daughter, who was all up in our conversation. "She's the only reason I'm here."

"You know you wanted to see me," he conceitedly added.

"Dad, she didn't want to see you." Ari grabbed her overnight bag from the car and tossed it toward her father's feet. "I had to beg her to pull up to the front. She was going to let me off at the corner. Now, can we go in the house? It's cold out here." She turned to me and waved. "Have fun at dinner, Mommy. I love you."

"Thank you, baby. I love you too."

Ari began ascended the steps toward the ranch-style home. She looked back at her father with her hand on her hip. He hadn't moved a muscle.

"Dinner, hunh? Who are you going to dinner with? Is that why you're so dressed up?"

Nessa went all out for her dinner. She sent out invitations requesting all white formal attire. I was always told that you don't wear white after Labor Day, but Nessa had me in a calf-length dress that hugged me just right. It was long-sleeved, and I topped it off with a silver and platinum fox fur collar. I had to throw some color in there somewhere.

"Dad!" Ari huffed. "Come on."

"Your daughter's calling you," I advised him. I reopened my door and slid down into the driver's seat. "Spend your time worrying about her, not me."

I closed the door and sped off. I spent more time over there than I expected to, and I was pushing it with the time. I pulled into Nessa's driveway with exactly three minutes to spare. I parked behind

Davina's car and carefully walked up the porch stairs in five-inch stilettos. I rang the doorbell twice before Nessa finally answered.

"You're late," she barked.

"I am not," I pulled my cell from my clutch to confirm the time. "It's 6:59. Sorry. I had to drop Ari off to her father."

"I'll give you a pass – this time. You, Ashley, and Davina are the only ones here anyway. Come on. We're all in the back."

I followed behind as Nessa led me through her spacious home. It was my first time there and I was in awe. Her place has a 'clinical' feel. Everything was white. Everything!

"You look nice by the way," she mentioned as she rounded a corner.

The compliment made me smile. "Thanks."

"Next time, follow directions. All white means all white."

She sure knew how to ruin a mood.

NESSA

My dinner was going well. Besides a few people who didn't understand the concept of time, everything was perfect. I wanted a chance to sit down and kick it with the girls I had grown to care for. Steele and I had been together for a number of years, and in a way, I considered everyone in attendance, family. I knew that my planned announcement during my vow renewal ceremony would take them for a loop. This dinner was my way of showing my appreciation before I exited stage left.

You see, my husband has a problem keeping his dick in his pants. He spent the entire five years that we dated and five years that we've been married entertaining other women. Normally, I'm not a weak bitch. Really, I'm not. It's just...Steele was all I knew. I was fifteen when we met, twenty when we got married, and now that I was leaning toward passing the quarter-century mark. I was done. I couldn't do it no more. I tried.

"What did you just say?" I questioned. Ashley's voice was so soft that I couldn't make out her words.

"I said," she repeated, much louder. "I'm going on the road with Reno. After the wedding, he has a few shows down south, and he's taking me with him."

You got a lot to learn, I thought to myself. Just like the rest of the St. John men, Reno had a wandering eye. He took women on the road before. They stayed behind while he did his thing. When they got tired, they left.

I scanned over the six women in attendance. Stephanie, Davina, and Shugg sat across from me as a trio. They quietly dug into their meals without much conversation. Ashley was at the far end – alone; which ironically was the same way she would be when she went on the road with Reno. Across from her, sat my childhood friend, Amy, and my younger sister, Leesey. My mother-in-law, Chandra, was a no-show due to babysitter duties. My egg donor was strung out somewhere, and Bliss still hadn't arrived. My eyes fell to the empty seat next to Ashley where Bliss was supposed to be sitting. I wondered what was taking so long. There was only one way to find out.

"Excuse me, ladies."

I stepped away from the table and entered my bedroom. Quickly glancing over my shoulder, I closed the door and stepped further into the room. Steele's actions had me in full blown stalker mode. Although I had already seen enough evidence to know that my suspicions were true, my curiosity had the best of me. I continued monitoring him without his knowledge. There were cameras discreetly placed all around the three homes that we owned. I could monitor any room, in any house, at any time of the day. I had the ability view real-time footage as it happened. I could also go back in time and review footage from the past. Technology made 'discreet' cheating damn near impossible. It didn't hurt that my husband felt that he was too smart to get caught. He thought that his mouthpiece was *that* damn good. I let him think I didn't know shit; while the whole time, I was collecting evidence to quit his ass for good. I was tired. Let me rephrase that...I was done. That's beyond tired, to the point of not giving a fuck anymore. At that moment, I just didn't give a fuck.

I tuned into the action. A scene was playing out right in our bedroom. Bliss wasn't there, but Steele sure was, along with the 'hoe of the day,' Chrysette. I knew all about her and her child. It was their situation that prompted me to orchestrate my own show and tell session. During my vow renewal ceremony, I was going to call Steele out and tell everyone in attendance exactly why I wasn't spending another year being Mrs. Steele St. John. He disrespected me privately by having other women in our house, so I was flipping the script, and embarrassing him in public. It was only right. I mean, *I* was the victim.

I heard her mention something about another baby, and I utilized the rewind function. She already had Steele believing he was the father of baby number one, even though the child looked nothing like him. That was another truth that I had the privilege of knowing. Steele wasn't the father of that girl. I could have disclosed my findings, but why do that? Why help him protect what he's worked for when he obviously didn't give a damn about what we built together? He was secretly peeling off money to the chick that was supposed to be going toward our future. Call me selfish, I don't care, but I hate having money taken from me. That's exactly what Steele was doing. He took from me, to give to some little bastard. It wasn't cool, and I wasn't putting up with it anymore.

Bliss' face came into view when after rewinding for a while. I pressed play to hear some of their conversation.

"Tell me what? What the hell is going on?" she asked.

"It ain't the first time," Steele admitted. "I got a daughter."

"What did you say?" Bliss took a step toward him and mugged his chest. "What the fuck did you just say, Steele?"

"You betta keep those hands to yourself, girl. You're gonna make me forget that you're my sister."

"You got a daughter? Steele...you have a fuckin' baby! What about Nes-" She paused before turning toward Chrysette. "You know what I mean."

Damn, I thought to myself. I assumed everyone in the family knew, and that they were just keeping it from me. Bliss' face displayed genuine shock upon hearing the news. I almost felt bad for putting her in that situation.

I fast-forwarded the video until I saw Bliss leave. I was satisfied when I saw the jewelry box in her hand. Checking the time on the video, I compared it to the current time. Twenty minutes had passed. Both Bliss and the photographer would be arriving any minute. The photographer was more so for me. I wanted a lasting memory of me and the girls before everything fell completely apart.

Quickly checking myself out in the mirror, I returned to my guests. It was one of the last nights we would all spend together, and the night was still young.

2

FEBRUARY 11TH

SHUGG

"What's wrong with you, Bliss?" I asked cautiously. She didn't seem like herself. I invited both her and Davina over for breakfast, and she had been in a slump since arriving.

"Nothing."

"Are you sure?"

"Yeah, I'm sure."

I watched her circle her food around her plate. She wasn't her usual, talkative self. I could feel something was wrong. I just couldn't let it go.

"It's something, Bliss. It's written all over your face. Maybe talking about it would help."

Her eyes fell to my left. Seated next to me was Cedric, stuffing his face as if he was having his last meal. It wasn't my intention to have him engaged in our conversation. He was headed out of the kitchen with his plate in hand, when Davina stopped him and asked about the bachelor's party. Cedric danced around the truth while easing down into the spot next to me.

"Cedric, baby, can you give us a minute?"

He looked up from his plate and went into negotiation mode. "Can I finish my breakfast first?"

"Of course, you can...in the bedroom."

"I see how it's gonna be," Cedric complained. He stood anyway and grabbed his plate with both hands. "A man can't even enjoy a meal without gettin' ordered around by a group of women."

"So dramatic," Davina teased.

"That's not being dramatic. That's being real. Men have feelings too, you know."

"Boy, go on!" I requested. "I'll take care of those 'feelings' later."

"In that case...you ladies enjoy the rest of your morning." Cedric picked up his pace as he disappeared from the room.

"Sorry, Bliss. He's a character when he wants to be." I looked over my shoulder to make sure he was gone. "Is that better? Now you can talk."

"There's not really much to say," Bliss began. She continued playing with her food and refusing to make eye contact. "It's just...you know how you think you know someone, only to find out you don't really know them at all."

"You're preaching to the choir!" I exclaimed. "Girl, that's the story of my life. Once a person reveals to me who they truly are, it's up to me to decide if I still want them in my life or not. That part can be hard; especially if a lot of time and energy has been invested."

"It's way more than that," Bliss admitted. "We're talking about family here."

"Family?" Davina questioned. She sat the half-empty cup of juice in her hand down on the table. "What's going on?"

"I probably shouldn't say anything."

"Well, you should have thought about that before you opened your mouth," Davina countered. "Spill it. Now I wanna know."

Bliss looked around as if she anticipated someone else walking in. Besides the three of us at the table, Cedric, Cree, and the little girl chilling in my stomach, we were the only people there.

"You started something. You can't take back," I teased.

Sitting back in my chair, I rubbed my stomach and watched Davina intently. She had both elbows on the table, waiting for Bliss to give her the tea. I chuckled as Bliss blatantly ignored her intense gaze. I studied their features. Although they weren't kin by blood, they were starting to resemble each other. Davina had lost a lot of weight thanks to Genesis working her out in both the gym and the bedroom, her words, not mine. Even her face was slimmer, which changed her look up drastically. Her hair fell in layers, which almost matched the layered bob Bliss was sporting. I guess the saying was true. When you hang around someone so long, you start to look like them.

"It's Steele," Bliss began reluctantly. She sat her fork down and ran her hands through her hair. "He's cheating on Nessa."

Davina and I shared a knowing look. This wasn't new information.

"O-kay," I hinted, hoping she would elaborate. "Why would that make you upset?" Luckily, she took the bait and continued.

"No, you don't understand. I'm talking about some serious shit." She leaned into the table and lowered her voice. "He has a daughter."

I gasped loudly and grabbed my chest with my hand. "What? A daughter? Are you serious, Bliss?"

Davina didn't look too surprised. She picked up her fork and began stuffing her face with her breakfast. Her appetite quickly picked up with a vengeance. Bliss noticed it too and called Davina out on it.

"You knew, didn't you?"

"What? No!"

I had been around Davina long enough to know that she was lying. Bliss, on the other hand, let it go without as much as questioning her.

"I can't believe it. I met the chick and everything," Bliss continued. "Steele is dead wrong. Nessa called me over this morning, and I didn't even want to go. How can I look her in the face knowing this information?"

"Sometimes it's just best to stay out of it," Davina added. "You didn't do anything wrong. Don't even put yourself in their situation."

Davina was right on the money with that one. Bliss didn't need get involved with anything that didn't concern her. That was Steele's problem. Although he was her brother, getting into his business would do more harm than good.

"I understand that," Bliss stated, grabbing her ringing phone. "I just don't want to seem like I'm two-faced. Steele is my brother, and I'm always gonna take his side, but as a woman, I feel bad for Nessa. Hold on real quick. Hello?"

Cedric reappeared with our bright-eyed son in his arms. As soon as Cree saw me, he whined and reached for me. I grabbed for my spoiled son and sat him in front of me.

"He's hungry. Do you want me to fix him some eggs or something? Or do you want to feed him?" Cree lifted up my shirt, answering his father's question for him. "Well, I guess he knows what he wants."

"I guess so."

Cedric strolled out, leaving us alone. I repositioned my son in my lap as Bliss stood to her feet.

"I gotta go, y'all."

"What? I thought we were chillin' for the whole day?" I complained. "Where are you going?"

Bliss walked over and softly squeezed Cree's cheek. "I know, but that's my dad. He called a meeting and I gotta be there. I'm sorry, Shugg. Next time, girl's day is on me."

"I'm gonna hold you to it," I mentioned as she grabbed her purse and keys. "Next week. No excuses!"

"Sure thing!" she said over her shoulder.

Just like that, she was out, downgrading our trio to a duo.

DAVINA

I finished my meal in silence. Bliss appeared distraught about the news and that made me feel like shit. I knew about Steele's daughter and had even seen her on a few occasions. Quite frankly, I thought the little girl was suspect. She didn't look anything like the mother, or Steele for that matter, but that didn't have anything to do with me. My husband told me not to say anything, and I respected his wishes.

"Does Nessa know?" Shugg questioned. I knew what she was talking about, but I played stupid anyway.

"Know what?"

"You know what I'm talking about, Davina. Does Nessa know about the baby?"

"What do you think?"

"Oh, shit. Damn. Steele ain't right."

"I know. It's a fucked-up situation, but Steele did it to himself. Nobody told him to fuck that girl. Genesis tried to talk to him, but he wouldn't listen. He's stubborn."

"What did Genesis say?" Shugg wanted to know details, as usual. She liked to have enough information to vividly paint a picture in her mind.

"He told him to get a DNA test. You remember how Shanelle and

Kita tried to get over on him, right? Well, he told Steele to get a test just to make sure. Steele said he didn't need one. He said he knows the little girl is his. He's been giving Chrysette money every month for over a year."

"Chrysette? Is that the girl's name?"

"Yeah, that's her. She's a young chick too."

"Sounds like a 'hoe' name," Shugg countered. "Fuckin' around with a married man. She should be ashamed of herself."

I loved my girl, but she could be hypocritical at times. I wasn't trying to be mean, but I had to put her in her place.

"People could say the same thing about you. Does 'Jett' ring a bell?"

"I didn't know he was married!"

"How do you know she did?"

Shugg paused and thought about it for a moment. I knew I was right, but Shugg would never admit it. Instead of accepting the truth, she quickly changed the subject.

"So, what do you want to do today? Since Bliss bailed on us, it's just me and you."

"Wanna catch a movie?" I suggested.

"Sure, as long as we're done before six. Cedric is making me go to a business dinner with him. It's gonna be so boring!"

"What about Cree? Is he going too?"

"Hell no! I'm hoping he'll act right, so we can take him back to Chandra. Bliss' son is still there, but Cree cried so bad, Cedric had to pick him up early this morning."

Chandra's face popped up in my head. My mother-in-law was stern and told it like it was, but that woman loved kids. If she called Cedric to pick Cree up, his behavior had to be out of the ordinary.

Shugg finished feeding her son, while I searched on my phone for a movie for us to watch. The selection wasn't the greatest, but there was another installment of the *Fifty Shades* trilogy playing. It was better than nothing.

"I found us a movie. The first showing starts in an hour and a half."

"Cool. Let me get this boy together and change into something else."

I migrated to the living room and made myself comfortable. I kicked my shoes off and plopped down on the couch. Shugg and I were close enough that I felt as if I were at home. Hell, being over her house was just like me being at home. The only thing missing was my hubby, Genesis. As his face came to mind, I pulled out my phone and called him.

"What's up, baby?" he said into the phone. I got all giggly and shit. I loved when my man called me 'baby.'

"Nothing, just thinking about you. Are you still home?"

"No. I'm headed to the club. Pops just called me."

"Wow. It must be important. Bliss just left too."

"I'll find out when I get there. Are you swinging by?"

It felt good to know I was always welcome. Genesis never kept anything from me, including family business.

"No. Shugg and I are going to the movies."

"A'ight. Have fun. Call me when you're done. I got something for you."

"What's that?" I asked with a smile.

"This dick."

"You're so nasty!"

"You like it."

Shugg still wasn't ready when I ended the call. I flipped through a few channels before I spread out across the couch. Eventually, the television began watching me.

"Davina!"

I woke up to see Shugg standing in front of me with her hand on her hip. "What?"

"I'm ready."

"Me too," I added sleepily. "Let's go."

"Well...come on then!"

Thankfully, Shugg drove. My short, thirty-minute nap took everything out of me. I was mentally and physically drained. It came on suddenly. I was fine one minute and tired as hell the next. My body did its own thing as of late. There wasn't anything I could do but deal with it.

"Are you alright?" Shugg asked, tapping me on my shoulder. "We're here."

I sat up in the passenger's seat and examined my surroundings. We were already parked at the theater.

"Yeah, I'm good," I mouthed.

Shugg exited the car, but my body didn't want to move. It wasn't until she came around to my side of the car and opened the door that I finally got out.

"You sure you ain't pregnant," Shugg teased. "I used to be tired all the time too. Then I found out I was having Cree."

I pressed on at the mention of a Cree's name. I suspected there was something going on, but I convinced myself otherwise. I just needed to relax and unwind. That was all. I had been going non-stop since returning from Miami. A good night's sleep would get me right. Being that Genesis was trying to 'poke' me every chance he got, it was almost impossible.

We went inside and purchased our tickets. Shugg decided to stop at the concession stand, and I followed behind.

"Do you want something?" she leaned over and asked me.

"Yeah, get me a salted pretzel, and..."

I paused for a moment and studied the two people to my far left. I couldn't stand either one of them, and I was surprised to see them together.

"And what?" Shugg asked with a sigh. "Come on now, Davina. You're holding up the line."

The mention of my name got the couple's attention. Disgraced attorney Stanley Weeks and Tranique whatever the hell her last name was now, had both eyes on me and Shugg. Childishly, I gave them the finger.

"Just the pretzel," I said with a smirk. "Unless Stanley and Tranique want something. They keep staring over here."

"What?" Shugg looked around in confusion until she saw exactly who I was talking about. "Shit. Why did I have to see her today? Look at me. I look terrible."

I scanned my girl. She wore a simple long-sleeved shirt and jeans. Her pregnant belly protruded forward, but she didn't look bad.

"Fuck her," I said, loud enough for everyone to hear. "Even on your worst day, that bitch ain't touchin' you."

Tranique had the balls to stroll over. She rolled her eyes at me and immediately started in on Shugg. "Well, well, well. If it isn't my husband's side bitch. Ooo, girl...life is taking a toll on your figure. Having Cedric around ain't all it's cracked up to be, hunh?"

"Actually," Shugg began, placing her hand on her hip. "Life's good. Brown Sugar is opening its third location, and as you can see," she rubbed her stomach confidently, "your *ex-husband* is working the hell outta this pussy. We're having our second baby."

Tranique couldn't hide the rage in her eyes. Shugg got under her skin. Tranique was expecting cool, calm, and collected Shugg. What she got, was a woman who didn't give a fuck.

"Come on, Stanley," Tranique hissed. "Let's go. They're not worth our time."

"Neither was your doctor," Shugg added. "Do you still got those bumps on your pussy or are they going away?"

Tranique's eyes widened like a deer caught in the headlights. She grabbed Stanley's hand and pulled him in the opposite direction. I laughed so hard I was damn near in tears.

"Why did you do that girl like that?" I asked.

"She tried it. Don't come for me when I know *all* your dirt! Every time I see her, I'm calling her ass out."

The face Shugg made told me she meant exactly what she said.

BLISS

"Hey, dad," I mouthed, walking into his office. His hand still gripped the doorknob when I leaned in for a hug.

"Bliss, what took you so long?"

"Traffic. I was out with Davina and Shugg when I got your call. I got here as fast as I could."

Glancing around, I noticed that all my brothers were in attendance. For the first time in forever, I was the late one.

Reno eased himself off the edge of our father's desk and strolled over to me. "What's up, sis?"

"Reno!" I practically threw myself at my baby brother. He was on the road so much, I hardly ever got to see him.

"Damn, girl. Are you tryin' to choke the shit out of me?" he complained.

I loosened my grip around his neck and apologized. "Sorry. I'm just so happy to see you. I saw your girlfriend last night, but you were a no-show."

"That's women shit, ya know. I was out with the fellas...but we'll talk. I'm here for the next few days."

I smiled at my brother, who eased into a plush chair adjacent from our father's desk. Directly across from him sat Emory, who greeted me with a head nod. My father, sat down in his leather chair, leaving the only available seat between Genesis and Steele. They sat on both sides of the leather couch, leaving the middle free for me. Weighing my options, I decided to hold up the wall.

"I know you're all probably wondering why I called you here," my father began in his deep baritone voice. "I'm glad you all showed up. Now, I only have to say this once. A lot of things are about to change, and…"

"Come on now, Pops," Steele interrupted. "Can we skip all this and get to the point? I got business waiting for me back home, if you know what-"

"The only business you care about is pussy, and that can wait." This time, it was me interrupting him. "Damn. Let him finish, why don't you?"

"What the fuck is your problem?" he snapped.

"Don't play stupid with me, Steele. I'm sure you remember what I walked in on yesterday." I gave him my 'come on nigga' look.

"What's she talking about?" Emory inquired.

"Nothing," Steele answered. "You know how Bliss is. Always blowing shit out of proportion."

"You would say some shit like that," I countered. "You're foul, Steele. Real foul."

"Somebody better start explaining themselves," my father huffed. "What the hell is going on? Anything we should all know about?"

"It's not my place to say." I crossed my arms over my chest. Steele was a grown man. If he wanted everyone to know he had a child, he should have been the one to tell them.

"Steele." My father turned to his oldest child and began rubbing his trimmed goatee. This meant he wanted answers. If Steele knew what was good for him, he would give our father what he wanted.

"It's nothing. She met Chrysette."

"That's it?" my father continued. "So, what's the problem?"

The confused look on Genesis Sr.'s face had me livid. I loved my father, but he was a man. A man who constantly cheated on our mother. Of course, he would be okay with Steele's behavior. Like father, like son.

"That's the problem!" I migrated to the middle of the room. "He has a wife at home."

"Shit happens, baby girl. That's life."

My father just didn't get it. I was a woman. I thought differently. I spent more time with Nessa than I did my own brother at times. I had to look my sister-in-law in the face knowing he was out there doing wrong.

"But that's not a reason for you to have an attitude with your brother," he continued. "He's your blood."

"You just don't understand." I returned to my position against the wall. Genesis abandoned his seat on the couch and stood next to me. Even in heels, his tall frame towered over me.

"He's right," Genesis agreed. When I rolled my eyes and smirked, he tapped my shoulder, regaining my attention. "It's not your business. All you can do is accept it and keep it moving."

"Would you be telling me the same advice if it were you and Davina? You two are married. If you had a baby on your wife, would you expect me to keep quiet and act like it's no big deal?"

"That's different, Bliss. You can't compare my actions to Steele's."

"Why not?"

"Because we're different people."

"Yeah, 'cause you done got soft," Steele interjected. He laughed to himself as if he had told the funniest joke in the world. "You got you a lawyer bitch and handed in your man card. She's calling the shots now."

"Nigga, you better find you somebody else to talk that shit to. Ain't nothin' about me soft."

"Alright, you two better stop that shit!" My father's voice boomed loudly, silencing the room. "We ain't here for that. Bliss, that's your brother. Despite his faults, he's still your brother. Agree with him. Disagree with him. I really don't give a damn, but he's family and always will be. That's between him and his wife. Steele and Genesis, chill with that shit. All five of you are gonna have to find a way to get along and work together. I am officially stepping down. I'm handing the club and everything along with it to all of you."

"What do you mean stepping down?" I questioned.

"I'm stepping down," he repeated. "I made a lot of money in this business. I met a lot of people and I think I made a good name for myself. Right now, I just want to sit back and reap the rewards. You only live once."

"You got caught up, didn't you?" Reno asked with a smirk. "Mom's making you do it, isn't she?"

Our father took a deep breath before answering. His sigh was all we needed to hear. We all burst out laughing, and just like that, we were good again.

"Yeah, she caught me. It was either give her what she wants or pack my bags. I damn sure ain't going nowhere."

I saw the same passion from my father's eyes in Steele's. He wasn't going anywhere either. He was content living a double life. Listening to my father made it all come together. Steele was having his cake and eating it too.

STEPHANIE

Why did my father choose today of all days to show up? He didn't tell me he was coming into town. He asked me how business was doing, and I told him the truth. His company took a big hit fourth quarter, but we were slowly recovering. We were barely six weeks into the new year. Financial recovery took time.

In true Danny Rivas fashion, he showed up on my doorstep and *told* me my plans for the evening. I was having dinner with both him and Cedric. We needed to discuss strategies for success and how to speed up the recovery process. Ari was still with her father, which took away my excuse as to why I couldn't attend. He waited for me to shower and slip into something dinner appropriate. We were chauffeured around town in his luxury rental, complete with a personal driver.

As soon as we arrived, I regretted being there. Cedric decided to bring Shugg, and I felt uncomfortable. If I had known we were bringing dates, I would have called my 'boy toy' Emory. He was some nice eye candy. I loved his caramel tone and slanted eyes. The only problem was, I had yet to disclose to my father that I was dating. Although I was a grown woman, I wasn't ready to open my personal life up to my father just yet.

"Stephanie," Cedric greeted me. I smiled genuinely but kept my distance. He stepped forward and hugged me as if we were old friends.

"It's nice to see you again, Cedric."

"The pleasure is all mine. I haven't seen you around the office. How've you been?"

My father and uncle owned Rivas Management Group, a financial firm with a growing list of high profile investors. Being the daughter of Danny Rivas secured my financial future, and I was content being a stay-at-home-mom and wife. My husband at the time was handed the job as the finance manager, but after allegations of infidelity, my father kicked his ass to the curb. I did too. We divorced a few months later. I stepped back into the company just to oversee things for a while. My father lived and worked out of the main office in New York and needed a trusting pair of eyes to look after things locally. Although Cedric had been promoted to finance manager, it wasn't the same as having *me* in the office.

"I've been good," I commented.

My eyes turned to Shugg standing at his side. She wore a simple black dress, that couldn't hide her growing baby bump. One of her hands grabbed it, while her other hand found Cedric's. She opened her mouth to speak, but I beat her to it.

"Good evening, Shugg."

"Hello, Stephanie," she said dryly. "You look lovely."

Of course, I do, I thought. Instead of dabbling in anymore unnecessary small talk, I turned around quickly checked us in. "Reservation for Rivas, please."

We were seated in the back of the restaurant. There was a private room that allowed for a more intimate setting. A round table sat in the middle of the small room, with seating for four. My father pulled my chair out for me, while Cedric did the same for Shugg. Our waiter poured us all a glass of complimentary champagne. Shugg pushed hers toward the center of the table.

"I'll just take a water please," she blushed. "I'm pregnant."

The middle aged man's face flushed in embarrassment. It was

apparent that he hadn't been paying attention. She wasn't just 'a little pregnant.' Her stomach was out there.

After ordering our meals, we ate and discussed strategies for next quarter. My father was determined to bring in some new business to counter a lucrative contract we had lost. It wasn't due to any error or fault on our part. The owner decided to sell, leaving Rivas Management Group with one less account to manage.

Cedric and my father began talking finance jargon that I didn't understand. I ate slowly, hoping Shugg wouldn't utilize the opportunity to spark up a conversation. Unfortunately, my ploy didn't work.

"So, how's Ari?" Shugg questioned across the table.

I took my time chewing my grilled asparagus. When I chewed exactly twenty-five times, I swallowed and finally answered her question. "She's doing well."

"That's great. Cree's doing well too. He's getting so big!"

Did I ask you about your son? I thought. Instead of saying what I was thinking, I simply smiled and nodded. I stuck a fork full of the baked fish from my plate into my mouth and diverted my attention to the waiter stepping toward us.

"How is everything? Can I get you anything else?"

"Everything is perfect as always!" my father boasted. "I think we're good right now but thank you."

The waiter waddled away with a cheesy grin on his face. My father was overexaggerating. The food was okay at best. I'd had better. Hell, I could cook better, and cooking wasn't my expertise.

"Are you excited about Nessa's wedding? Well, vow renewal," Shugg continued.

She just had to say something. Why couldn't she just sit there and shut the hell up? I didn't understand it. Why would she want to talk to me? Besides fucking the same man, we had nothing in common.

"Yes, I am. I'm honored to have been asked to witness their union."

"Me too. I'm sure it's going to be beautiful."

"Any time two people stand before God and vow to love, honor, and cherish each other, it's beautiful. Marriage is sacred."

That shut her up. She didn't have a comeback for that one. Maybe it was because she felt guilty about sleeping with a married man. Then again, maybe not. Oh well. The only thing I did know was that Shugg was momentarily quiet and I was able to finish my meal. It lasted all of a few minutes.

"Are you going with Emory?"

"Emory?" my father questioned, exiting his conversation and entering mine. "Who's Emory?"

"Emory St. John," Shugg clarified. "He's the brother of my friend's husband."

"And what does that have to do with you, Stephanie?" my father inquired.

I felt like a child once again. My hands began to sweat under his intense gaze. "We're, umm...dating."

"Dating? Why is this my first time hearing about this?"

I cut my eyes at Shugg. She ran her big mouth and started something that didn't concern her in the least bit.

"It's still new, dad."

"We'll talk," he mentioned quietly.

Great, I thought. Thanks to Shugg, I had to hear my father's mouth the whole ride home.

NESSA

"What's wrong?" Steele asked, walking up behind me.

"Nothing."

I turned my phone upside down, hiding the picture displayed on the screen.

"It's gotta be something. What's up? Talk to me?"

He snatched the phone from my hand and viewed my sister's ultrasound picture. It was her way of disclosing to me that she was pregnant, but Steele didn't know that. He assumed it was mine.

"Are you pregnant?" he questioned in horror.

"No, I'm not."

"So, what's this?" He handed the phone back to me.

"It's Leesey's. She just found out today. She's seven weeks."

"Whew," Steele exhaled, brushing his hand across his forehead. "I was nervous there for a minute."

"We've been married for five years. Why would that make you nervous?"

"Nessa, we've already talked about this. I'm too selfish to have a baby. The only person I want to share my time with is you, and only you. I ain't 'bout to be chasin' after no kid."

He wrapped his arms around me, pushing me back onto the bed.

He began kissing the side of my face, while his hands explored my body. I tried to push him off me, but our difference in weight gave him the advantage.

"I wouldn't have a child with you even if you wanted one."

He stopped kissing me and peered at me questioningly. "What do you mean by that?"

"Nothing."

Steele leaned back but didn't break the gaze. He seemed to be confused by my words. I wanted to give him a piece of my mind, but I kept my mouth shut. I had to keep up the front for three more days, and then he would know exactly how I felt.

"Oh, you meant something. So, you're telling me if I wanted a baby, you wouldn't give me one? What kinda shit is that?"

"Who gave you the power to call the shots? Why do we have to have a baby only if *you* want one? If it doesn't matter what I want, it shouldn't matter what you want."

"But you don't want a baby either."

I don't know what came over me. One moment I was fine and standing my ground. The next moment I was crying my eyes out.

"Don't tell me what I want."

I turned my body and rolled out from under him. He reached for me, but I was already off the bed and on my feet.

"You buggin'. It must be that time of the month."

"Funny," I mouthed, turning my nose up in irritation. "You don't know shit. My period was last week. Maybe you're getting me confused with someone else."

I entered the bathroom and slammed the door. I plopped down on the toilet and buried my face in my hands. The tears flowed immediately, and I let them fall. Steele was dead wrong for what he was doing to me. For years, I stood by his side and catered to his every need. I thought I was being a good wife. Then, my woman's intuition kicked in. I could 'feel' that something was wrong. It was like...I didn't have proof, but I just knew something was going on. When I got proof, I stayed anyway. People probably looked at me and thought I was the dumbest female in the world. I know I would have. How could I stay with a man who repeatedly gave himself to other women? The problem was, I didn't have a plan B. Steele was all I knew. I had been with him so long that I had become comfortable. I loved and hated him at the same damn time.

It wasn't until my heart-to-heart with Davina that I decided to do better. She didn't do it intentionally, but she did make me see that I was settling when I didn't have to. I heard her talking about a case that she won and how the wife is now set for life. I asked questions about other cases and listened intently. I learned that leaving Steele would not force me to walk away empty-handed. Oh no! I was entitled to maintain the same lifestyle that I had been living. It wasn't my fault that Steele fucked up. That was on him, and I didn't have to suffer for his misdeeds. In fact, I would be good no matter what.

That's when I came up with my plan. Valentine's Day was coming up and the day of love was the perfect day to part ways with the man who had caused me so much pain. Just like I didn't see it coming, I didn't want Steele to see it coming either. I asked him about renewing our vows, and he was all for it. He even spent a nice piece of change putting everything together on such short notice. Too bad for him, he was going to lose a lot more than he bargained for. Until then, I had to play it cool.

Steele entered the bathroom behind me. When he saw me crying, he knelt down in front of me. I knew what I had to do, but that didn't stop it from hurting. Deep down inside, I loved Steele. I wished things could have been different. If I had my way, I would remain his wife and live happily ever after. I wanted to be with him. I wanted my marriage. I wanted to have his kids, but life didn't work the way I wanted it to. I wasn't going to tolerate sharing a man. Steele's actions made it perfectly clear that he wasn't going to change. If I couldn't be the only one, I wasn't going to be with him at all. It was simple as that.

"Nessa, baby, I'm sorry," he whispered.

"Just go on, Steele."

"No, let's talk about this. I don't like to see you cry."

He removed my hands from my face and peered at me lovingly. He could be sweet when he wanted to, and that was something I was going to miss. If only he could have been the man that he vowed to be. Wiping my face with the back of his hands, he sat up on his knees and faced me.

"Nessa, I love you. Please, don't cry."

That made me cry more. Why lie to me in my face? If he loved me, he wouldn't be planning baby number two with his mistress. Loving me didn't mean hurting me. That's exactly what he was doing.

"Don't lie to me."

"I'm not lying. Baby, we got three more days before I walk down that aisle again and marry you for the second time. If I didn't love you, I wouldn't be doing it. I'm sorry for upsetting you; I just thought we were on the same page as far as kids were concerned. I don't want to see you cry. I only want to see you happy. If having a baby is something you want, maybe we can talk about it somewhere down the line. Right now, I just want to enjoy being with you. Is that too much to ask?"

"No," I said, regaining my composure. I had a brief moment of weakness, but I got myself together.

"Good. Put your shoes on," Steele demanded. He stood to his feet and stared down at me. "I wanna take you somewhere."

"Where?" I questioned.

"Somewhere. It's a surprise."

With a boyish smile, he extended his hand to me. I took it and allowed him to pull me to my feet.

"Steele, you know I don't like surprises."

"You'll like this one. I promise."

Little did he know; his promises didn't mean shit to me anymore.

3

FEBRUARY 12TH

SHUGG

"Scoot over!" I complained, pushing Cedric away from me. "You're gonna roll on top of Cree!"

The mention of our son's name had Cedric sitting up in the bed. He looked around sleepily until he noticed Cree laying comfortably in the middle of our king-sized bed. Cedric sighed loudly and ran his hand over the deep waves in his head.

"Shugg...What's he doing in the bed? We said we weren't gonna do this. I don't want him getting comfortable laying in here with us. He has his own bed and his own room."

"I know, but he keeps crying. I'm tired of going back and forth trying to calm him down. I think he's teething again. You're over there knocked out; sleeping good. I'm tired, Cedric. If being in our bed will keep him quiet, then our bed is where he's sleeping tonight."

"The hell he is."

Cedric hopped up, pulling Cree up with him. Our son opened his eyes, but quickly closed them again as he snuggled against his father's bare chest. Cedric disappeared through the doorway and returned without Cree.

"See, that's how you do it. You gotta be firm, Shugg. You gotta let him know who's the boss. I told him he was sleeping in his bed and look where he's at. He's in his bed."

"How long do you think that's gonna last?" I quizzed.

"All night." Cedric eased into the bed behind me and wrapped his arms around me. "We gotta get this under control now. Our baby girl will be here soon. Ain't no way in hell I'm sleeping with two kids in the bed with me."

"I know," I mumbled. It was hard standing my ground when every time Cree cried, my breasts turned into hydrants. They leaked uncontrollably at the sound of his voice.

Twenty minutes later, they were doing just that. Cree started crying again, and I jumped to the rescue.

"No, no," Cedric said with assertion. "I'll get him."

Cree slept in the bed with us. After being fed, he fell into a peaceful sleep right next to me. Cedric migrated toward the edge, giving us more space. He didn't complain further; although having Cree in the bed meant there would be absolutely no sex.

By sunrise, Cedric was singing a different tune. The smell of bacon and eggs had my mouth salivating before I was out of the bed. I rose to find Cree scooting toward the edge. My big boy smelled the food too!

I picked Cree up and walked into the kitchen. Cedric was wearing only a pair of fitted boxers as he worked his magic on the stove. He was humming a song loudly, which had me giggling in the doorway.

"Shit!" He yelled, catching a glimpse of me out of the corner of his eye. "Girl, you scared the hell out of me. Don't be walking up on me when I'm exercising my vocals."

"Is that what that was," I teased, packing Cree on my hip. "It sounded more like a wounded dog crying out for help."

"Very funny."

He leaned down and kissed me when I approached him. He had a frying pan in his hand, with two fried eggs ready to be flipped. My eyes found a nearby plate already filled to capacity. It was more food than all three of us could have eaten together. I stared at it questioningly, while grabbing a piece of bacon.

"Are you expecting company?"

"Yeah, Genesis is coming by. I think Davina might be rolling through as well."

"Really? Why?"

"To get Cree. As a matter of fact, go ahead and feed him now. If you need to pump or do any of that shit, you gotta do it before they get here."

Cree wasn't worried about my titties. He was too busy trying to steal the bacon from my hands. I tore off a little piece and gave it to him.

"Why? Where's he going?"

"With his godparents. You know Genesis has been wanting a baby. We need a break, and he's trying to get Davina in the mood to give him one. He thinks that having Cree around for the afternoon might give her baby fever."

"Shit, or it'll make her not want a baby at all," I interjected. "Cree is high-strung. He needs a lot of attention."

"They'll figure that out. It has nothing to do with us. Okay. We're about to get a break. Let's just enjoy it."

"A break?" I questioned, raising an eyebrow. Cree eyed the bacon on the counter and I tore him off another piece. "What kind of break?"

"A whole break," Cedric confirmed. "A whole day to do whatever we want. I hope you're ready."

He scooped the eggs from the frying pan and added them to the plate. Sitting the pan in the sink, he turned his attention to me and slapped the back of my ass.

"Ow!"

"You're gonna be saying more than that in about an hour."

"Oh, really?" I challenged.

"Damn right. Just wait and see. All this shit I cooked is for y'all. My breakfast is right there." He pointed toward my pussy. "I ain't had breakfast in a minute. I'm long overdue."

If I had panties on, they would have been slick with my juices. I loved when Cedric talked nasty to me. It made me all hot and bothered. Shit...What time was it? What was taking Genesis so long?

Quickly, I fixed Cree a plate of eggs, one piece of bacon, and disappeared into the bedroom to get him ready. I had sex on my brain, and I wasn't thinking straight. The boy damn near choked on the food that I had failed to cut up. Luckily, I caught myself as he tried to stuff the entire strip of bacon in his mouth.

"Boy, slow down!" I ranted. "Stop being so damn greedy."

Cree looked back at me as if I were the crazy one. At that moment I was. Crazy and horny. It wasn't a good combination. Genesis needed to hurry up.

DAVINA

I was supposed to ride out with Genesis, but I felt like sleeping in. We would be going back to Miami soon, and once there, sleep would be damn near impossible. I ran two separate law firms, but my Miami firm was much more profitable. I dealt with high-profile clients who brought in the big bucks. With money, came whiney, demanding people, who felt that their case was the most important one on my caseload. Going to Miami was like walking into the lion's den; it was always busy, and I stayed on my toes.

In addition to the law firms that I owned, I helped Genesis with Head Bangerz II. It was a gentleman's club that catered to the rich and famous. I helped him from afar, until I saw how much pussy was thrown at him on a daily basis. That's when I started making my presence known. Sometimes you had to show up, so hoes wouldn't show out. Genesis was my man, and I'd be damned if a half-naked bitch stepped in and took what I had invested my time and energy into. It wasn't happening.

I rolled over in bed when I heard the front door open. My big dick hubby was back, and I was ready to be long-stroked. I got on all fours and hiked my ass up in the air, so he could see exactly what I was working with. He liked that 'easy access' shit.

"As tempting as that is, baby," Genesis began, "I'ma have to pass right now. We got company."

My neck whipped around to see who was with him. Cree smiled at all my naked glory. He was a baby, so he was cool. He wouldn't remember shit anyway; which is why I took my time crawling out of bed.

"Hold on," I warned, reaching for my robe. "I didn't know you were bringing him with you."

"That was the point. I wanted to surprise you," Genesis mentioned, visibly amused by my nakedness.

He placed Cree on the bed and helped me tie the belt for my robe. He also squeezed both my breasts and my ass as I reached for *my* baby.

"Cree!" I boasted, falling on the bed beside him. "Auntie missed her baby."

"Well, I'll leave you two alone," Genesis said with a smile. "I gotta go to the club and check on a few things. Do you need anything before I go?"

"Hmm...What do you have up your sleeve, Genesis?"

"Nothing. Shugg needed a break. Who better to give it to her than you? You are the godmother."

"Or us." I shot back. "And you are the godfather."

"You're right. That's no problem. Put some clothes on. We'll all roll out together."

"No," I paused, moving Cree onto my lap. "He doesn't need to be in a titty bar. He sees enough of that with Shugg."

"Well, he should be right at home then. If you've seen one, you've seen them all. You wanna go to Head Bangerz Cree?"

It was as if the little boy knew what Genesis was saying. He became hyper in my lap, determined to escape from my loose grip. He was definitely a titty baby. There was no doubt about that.

"Calm your mannish behind down, boy," I preached, referring to the terminology my grandmother used to use on my brother. "You got plenty of time for that."

I sent Genesis on his way and chilled with Cree solo. We had fun for a while, but I quickly became bored being in the house. Genesis had everything for me; car seat, stroller, playpen, and even an overly packed diaper bag. I showered and changed with Cree playing quietly inside his playpen. When I was done, I slipped into a pair of jeans, a thick sweater, and a pair of *Uggs* that matched the same style Cree had on his feet. I spoiled my godson rotten.

Our first stop was my office. There were a few things I needed to sign off on, and it would be easier to do it in person. Also, it gave me a chance to sneak up on my staff to see how they acted in my absence.

"Mrs. St. John," my receptionist, Sharon acknowledged as I stepped through the door. "I mean, Davina. I'm sorry. How are you this afternoon?"

"I'm fine, Sharon." I pushed the strolled up to her desk, giving her an opportunity to see my pride and joy. "We're just out and about. How are things here?"

"They're great," Sharon boasted. She smiled tenderly and ran her fingers through her short, salt-and-pepper hair. She was an older woman and had been in the legal business for some time. "I have those documents for you to sign."

"Great. Get them ready for me and I'll be right back. I'm gonna go and say 'hi' to everyone.

I picked Cree up out of his stroller and walked with him on my hip to everyone's office. They all gushed over him. I heard from several people how cute he was; which was true. I also managed to handle business and still keep my sanity - all with him in tow. After signing the required documents, I left and took Cree to get something to eat. There was a sandwich shop down the street, and a park not too far from it. We ate a light lunch and hung out by a small pond. It was warm for a February day, and Cree got so tickled throwing bread toward the ducks.

When one of the big ducks, goose, or whatever the hell it was got a little too close, I instantly went into mommy mode. I picked Cree up off the wooden bench and stood my ground. The bird lowered its head and started charging toward me. I hightailed it up out of there with Cree tucked under my arms. That damn bird finished off the rest of my sandwich that fell to the ground in my hasty departure.

As bad as I wanted that sandwich, I wanted to protect Cree more. He was all that I was worried about at that moment, and if I had to, I would have squared up with that damn bird. Luckily, it was over just as quick as it started. Cree was oblivious to what *could* have happened.

"You okay, Cree?" I asked, strapping him back into his car seat. He looked at me and smiled like he did every time I said his name. "Of course, you are. Auntie Davina is the shit."

When he smiled again, I kissed him on the cheek. He made a few sounds in his 'baby talk' and blew spit bubbles at me.

"I love you too, Cree," I mouthed. "I can't wait to have a little boy just like you."

I caught myself, but it was too late. I had already spoken it into existence.

BLISS

"What's your problem, Bliss?" my mother asked.

"Nothing."

"Are you sure? You're not acting like yourself."

"Yes, I'm sure. Well, actually...No...Yes...Ugh... I'm sure."

"What is it?"

I sat on the edge of her bed watching her reorganize one of her dresser drawers. She was a stickler for things being perfect. If anything was out of place, she'd know it, and stop what she was doing just to put it back in its rightful place. Pausing momentarily, she waited for my response.

"Really, it's nothing."

"Are you forgetting that I carried you forty-one weeks, only to be in labor twenty-seven hours, eighteen minutes, and only God knows how many seconds. I know you, Bliss. I also know when something is on your mind. If you didn't want to talk about it, you wouldn't be over here moping around. Now...what's going on?"

"It's your oldest child."

"Okay. And what's going on with Steele?"

"He should be the one to tell you." I crossed my legs and intertwined my fingers in my lap. A concerned look spread across her face. "That is, if you don't already know."

My mother was the epitome of a real woman. She did everything with style and grace – including handling her cheating husband. It was no secret that my father's eyes wandered more than just a little bit. From the outside looking in, it may have seemed like my father was getting away with entertaining other women. Only a fool would think that. When it was all said and done, Chandra St. John called the shots. My father simply played his part.

"Out with it."

I closed my eyes and gave her the information she requested. "Mom, Steele has a baby...and another one on the way."

I paused to gauge her reaction. She shook her head and resumed reorganizing her drawers.

"That damn boy. He's never gonna learn."

The way she spoke implied that she already knew. I raised an eyebrow and questioned her further.

"Did you already know, too?"

"Of course, I knew, Bliss. Do you really think Steele would have a baby and not tell me? He's my son."

"So, it was just me. I was the only person that didn't know."

"Bliss, you know how you are. Why would Steele tell you when all you're gonna do is chastise him?"

"I should've known you would take his side. It's no secret he's your favorite."

I stood from my seat and adjusted my cargo pants around my waist. I paired them with black pumps and a cutoff sweatshirt.

"Sit down," my mother demanded.

I did what I was told and sat my ass down. Chandra wasn't against knocking some sense into her children. Her hands were just as lethal as her mouth.

"Ain't nobody taking no damn side. You're just in your fuckin' feelings. You better get out of that shit, and quick. Steele don't owe you nothing."

"He owes it to his wife!" I declared. "Why is everybody acting like this is okay?"

"Exactly! So why are *you* mad?"

That was a good question. Why was I mad? Well, I was a woman, and as a woman, I felt bad for Nessa.

"Because," I began, but my mother quickly cut me off.

"Because? Because what? Because you're a female? Because you got a pussy instead of a dick? You know I give it to you straight, Bliss. I love you, just like I love my four other kids. None of you are perfect, including you. If my memory serves me correctly, Steele ain't the only one who's keeping a secret." To add insult to injury, she continued, looking at me skeptically. "How's Ty doing? Is he going to the vow renewal ceremony?"

"Of course, he is," I asserted. "Where else would he be?"

"I don't know." She placed a folded pair of socks back in the drawer and gave me her undivided attention. "Maybe the same place he was when you were making *your* child. He sure as hell wasn't there."

I wasn't listening to my mother's shit anymore. I made *one* mistake during my relationship with Ty and she threw it in my face. It wasn't right, and I wasn't standing for it.

"You're so quick to point out my faults but you worship the ground Steele walks on. That's bullshit! I'm out of here!"

I stood to leave, but she blocked my path. Her frame was small and petite, but something about her stance made me think twice before trying her.

"Why are you leaving, Bliss? Hunh? You don't wanna hear the truth? You're too busy faulting Steele when you did the same damn thing. When are you gonna tell Ty his son might not be his? Better yet, when are you gonna tell him that you fucked his friend? When are you gonna do that, Bliss? Want me to call him? I will! And when you do, I'll tell Steele to come clean to Nessa."

"This ain't about me," I hissed through gritted teeth.

"Just like it ain't about Steele. You're wrong just like he is, but you don't see me all up in your ass. No. I let you live your life just like I let

Steele live his. As far as Nessa goes, she's a grown ass woman. Unlike Ty, that girl ain't stupid."

"What do you mean by that?" I became defensive as I brought my hands to my hips. "My man ain't stupid."

"Your son and his friend could pass for twins and Ty is still claiming him as his own. Something's wrong with that boy. He's stupid. Hell, even Nessa would have picked up on that."

I sucked my teeth and sighed loudly. I didn't want to disrespect my mother, but her words were pissing me off. Ty wasn't stupid, dumb, or whatever else she might have been thinking. He was my man, and I loved him. It wasn't his fault. I made a mistake, and because of that, I kept close tabs on him. I never meant to have a baby by his friend. That was never the plan. I was just mad at Ty for staying out all night. It was a one-time thing. Well, twice. Okay...three times, but it didn't happen again. We both realized that we were wrong and decided to take our secret to the grave. Then, I had my son. With each passing day, he looks more and more like his biological father.

"Look," my mother continued, softening her tone. "I'm not trying to beat up on you or upset you. I just want you to see how hypocritical you're being. Don't fault Steele but make excuses for yourself. That ain't right. Don't feel sorry for Nessa either." My mother crossed her arms over her chest and continued. "That girl has more power than you think. Once she realizes that, Steele will be at *her* mercy."

STEPHANIE

My dad went off on me. He let me know exactly how he felt, without any regard for my feelings. He told me that I was moving too fast, even though I left Jett alone over a year prior.

"Too fast? That's a little far-fetched, don't you think? I'm divorced, not dead. At the end of the day, I'm still a woman."

"Remember who you're talking to," he warned.

"I'm sorry. I'm not trying to be disrespectful, but you act like I'm still a child. Dad, I'm a grown woman with a child. I can date whoever I want. I don't need your approval. We're just getting to know each other and having fun. Is that so bad?"

"That's what I'm worried about," he sighed. "Fun leads to bad decisions. You got a daughter, Stephanie. My granddaughter should be your number one priority. You don't need to bring anyone else into her life."

"Dad, you're being ridiculous."

He spared me the lecture after arriving home from our business dinner. I thought I had dodged a bullet. That was, until he called for me to join him for a late lunch. Everything was fine. We ate and had a good time together. He chose the ride home to question me about my relationship. The driver rounded the corner and arrived at my place.

Stopping in front, the car was shut off, and I turned to my father giving him my parting words.

"I love you, Dad. I know you want the best for me, but you're being overprotective. I haven't been a little girl for some time. You trust me to run your business, so you should trust me to run my own life."

"I trust you. It's him I don't trust."

"But you don't know him."

"I don't have to know him. I still don't trust him. He's a man and men only want one thing." My father gave me 'the look,' expecting me to understand. I understood alright. Danny Rivas was just as crazy as he was overbearing.

"Well, he already got that, and he's still around. I guess that's not all he wanted after all."

"Stephanie Ann Rivas!"

I chuckled and grabbed for the door handle. "Dad...stop being so narrow-minded. His name is Emory. He's good to me, and Ari adores him."

"He's already met my granddaughter?!"

"Yes, he has, and she's fine with him, Dad. You should be too. Trust me...I wouldn't bring just anyone around Ari."

The car sped off after I stepped out. My relationship was something he was going to have to get used to. The best way for him to do that was to meet the man responsible for my newfound happiness.

Later that evening, he called and requested just that. He wanted to have a sit down with Emory and feel him out. I agreed to set it up, just to get him off the phone, but my father was demanding and used to getting his way.

"Tonight. I can be by your place at five."

"Tonight," I repeated with hesitation. "That's short notice, Dad. How about we check our schedules and get back to you? I was thinking more like the next time you visit."

"No, today. I won't feel right until I meet this man. Are you trying to send me to an early grave?"

"No, Dad," I joked. "I'll see what I can do. I won't make any promises, though. You're not giving me much time."

I ran the idea past Emory, who agreed without hesitation. "Sure, I'll meet your Pops. Tonight, you said?"

"Yeah. Are you sure that's okay? I mean...I can reschedule for a later date."

"It's cool," he reaffirmed. "Tonight, it is."

With Ari gone, Emory and I used her absence to our advantage. He stayed the night with me for the first time and kept me up for all of it. We fucked until we were tired of fucking; and for us, that was hard to do. Emory might have been younger than me, but my stamina was right up there with his. I matched both his speed and rhythm, as he broke me off what I couldn't get enough of.

The 'L-word' hadn't officially been thrown out there, but I sensed it was coming. He treated me better than I had ever been treated before and the way things were going, I would be reciting it in no time. Or shouting it. Emory had that effect on me. He hit *that* spot, and I let out a moan comparable to a sharp soprano. My body was sent into a wave of convulsions as Emory taunted me during my orgasm.

"That's what I do. Yeah, let that shit out. Don't hold back."

I let him have his fun. I was stuck in my orgasmic high. I couldn't do anything anyway. When my legs stopped shaking, and my insides shopped thumping, it was my turn to physically drain *him*. I threw it back, rocking back and forth on his stiff pole. He tightened his grip on my waist to slow the pace, but I was in control. At that moment, it was *my* dick.

"Aww, shit. I'm 'bout to cum."

Usually, I would take that cue and get on all fours. Emory was a freak and liked to squirt his warm load all over my titties and shit. Unfortunately, that wasn't the case. He wanted to keep running his mouth, so I kept working my ass.

"Stephanie...Slow damn...Shit..."

I quickened my pace. Slowing down wasn't an option. He should have thought about that before he opened his mouth. As his body stilled, I continued working my ass and hips in a circular motion.

"You ain't right," Emory said after a long pause. His breaths were labored, and his forehead was covered with sweat. Carefully, he removed the condom and tossed it in the trash.

Playfully, I pushed his chest, only to start a weak wrestling match right there in the bed. After that, we showered and cuddled up in each other's arms.

Emory went home to change as I rummaged through my closet to find something to put on. My father was already working on his second drink when Emory returned. My baby walked through the door, and my dad stood to greet him.

"Dad, this is Emory. Emory, this is my dad, Danny Rivas."

"It's nice to meet you," Emory stated, extending his hand. "Stephanie talks a lot about you."

"Oh, really."

My father rubbed the trimmed goatee on his face as he took Emory in. He was well-dressed, like I coached him to be. His designer suit and round-top loafers rivaled the same style worn by my father, and my father's nod was exactly what I wanted to see. He approved. As we migrated toward the seating area, Emory surprised me by sparking up a conversation about sports.

"So, Mr. Rivas, Stephanie tells me you're a *Giants* fan."

I gave Emory a questioning look. I told him no such thing, but a simple search of Google would show how much of a die-hard fan my father was.

"Yes, I am. I've been a season ticket holder for years. I just wish they'd get it together."

"Tell me about it," Emory countered. "My Pops knows the GM, and he's just as frustrated as everyone else. He's ready to clean house."

"That wouldn't be such a bad thing."

They walked off without me, continuing their conversation about boring ass football. It was a good sign. Emory was winning my father over.

NESSA

"Close your eyes," Steele requested.

We'd been driving all night and well into the morning. My body ached and the feeling of having to use the bathroom for the third time was slowly creeping up on me.

"I don't have time for games, Steele. I'm not closing my eyes. Where the hell are we?"

I was beyond tired. The only way I was closing my eyes was if I had a comfy bed to lay down in.

He pulled our car over and parked on the side of the road. Realizing that we weren't going anywhere had my irritation at an all-time high.

"We ain't going nowhere until you close your eyes."

To emphasize his point, he cracked his window and shut the car off. I couldn't believe what he was doing. Steele was so fucking stubborn. Why couldn't he just tell me where we were going?

"Steele, come on. Stop playing. We're gonna get hit. Let's go!"

"That's a risk we're gonna take. I ain't starting this bitch back up until your eyes are closed. I told you...it's a surprise."

"We're in California?" I stated with an attitude. "Surprise."

I didn't know what city we were in, but I saw the 'Welcome to

California' sign miles ago. I didn't question it at first. Steele and I had made trips to California before, but it was usually to pick up a package or two. I had the route damn near memorized, but the path Steele was on didn't lead to Humboldt County.

"No shit," he barked.

"Don't get a damn attitude with me. I didn't do shit to you. You want me to close my fuckin' eyes and I don't even know where the hell I am. Are you about to do something to me? Shit, are you gonna take me through one of these sand dunes and blow my fuckin' brains out?"

"You're crazy as hell. Why the fuck would I do that?"

"I don't know, but nothing about you surprises me anymore." I crossed my arms over my chest and sighed loudly.

"What do you mean by that?" He appeared genuinely hurt.

Seeing the confusion on his face almost tugged at my heart. *Almost.* If I didn't know any better, I would have fallen for those puppy dog eyes staring back at me. Since I did know better, I just let it go. *Two more days*, I thought.

"Nothing. Forget I said anything."

I perched my feet up on the dashboard. It was tacky, and a little hillbilly-ish, but oh well. We weren't going anywhere. I might as well get comfortable.

"Nessa," Steele spoke. "Do you trust me?"

Hell no, my inner voice spoke. I wouldn't trust his ass even if he took a bath in holy water. Sticking with my plan, I mouthed, "Yes."

"Close your eyes, then."

I glanced out the window. Steele wasn't budging. Standing my ground wasn't going to get me anything but a wet seat if I didn't concede. I silently prayed that my husband wasn't on no funny shit and allowed my eyes to fall shut.

"What the fuck?" I felt something wrap around my face.

"It's a blindfold. I wanna make sure your eyes are closed."

He put the car in motion once again. We drove so long, I was tempted to remove the blindfold myself. A host of crazy thoughts went through my head as each minute passed. I was convinced that Steele was about to kill me. It was taking way too long.

"I'm taking this blindfold off."

"No, don't. Five more minutes."

I huffed loudly and agreed. "Fine."

Moments passed before I felt a hand caressing the soft curls I had created the day before. It was something Steele did often. For some reason, he loved to play in my hair. When his fingers grazed the top of my ear, he spoke.

"You are so beautiful."

"Thank you," I responded flatly.

"You don't have to thank me but sit tight. We're here."

I could hear him exit the driver's side. Seconds later, my door was opening, and he slowly helped me out.

"It's okay. I got you," he reassured, guiding me to my feet.

Allowing him to be my eyes, I held onto him tightly. We walked for a little over a minute before the texture of the ground underneath my feet changed. It wasn't hard, like pavement anymore. It was soft, and my feet sunk with every step.

"Steele, what is that?"

"You trust me, remember?"

I told him I did, and that's all that mattered. I concentrated on each step, making sure that I didn't fall. A few times, I stumbled, and Steele eased me back upright. Finally, we came to a complete stop.

"I'm gonna take the blindfold off, but keep your eyes closed."

I did as I was told and stood there nervously with my eyes squeezed shut. It took forever for Steele to tell me to open my eyes, but when he did, I saw the most beautiful view that I had ever seen.

"This is Coronado Beach," Steele explained.

I was too caught up in the beauty of it all. It was perfect; glistening sand, blue water, and a huge building with a unique, but historic appeal. I walked toward the water, with Steele right on my heels.

"Wow. It's so pretty."

"It is, isn't it? I saw this place a few years ago. I remember coming here and thinking that you'd love it. It's the perfect place to do it all over again, you know."

"Do what?" I eyed him suspiciously, pulling at the crop top exposing my bare stomach. It was February after all, but I was dressed to watch *Netflix* and chill.

"Six years ago, on this very day, I asked you to marry me. Remember that?"

I smiled at the memory. He was never good with dates, but he remembered the day he asked me to be his wife.

"How can I forget? It was one of the best days of my life. I told you I loved the water, but since we didn't live close to a beach or anything, you proposed at the lake. Remember the people fishing and looking at us like we were crazy? I was so embarrassed."

He flashed a boyish grin that brought back memories. Times sure had changed. I thought that I would spend the rest of my life with Steele. In a couple days, life with him as I knew it would be over.

"I hope this makes up for it?"

"What?"

Reaching in his pocket, he produced a ring box and opened it. He lowered himself to one knee, but I couldn't take my eyes off the rock sparkling in front of me.

"Nessa St. John, will you marry me...again?"

I was tempted to say 'No,' but I was no fool. That ring was mine.

"Yes."

He slid my wedding set off the ring finger of my left hand and placed it on the ring finger of the right. The new ring was placed on my left hand. Surprisingly, it didn't feel heavy, although it had to be at least double the carat size of my original ring. I held my hand up in front of my face and admired my new gift. If only things were different.

4

FEBRUARY 13TH

SHUGG

"*I*'m the luckiest man in the world," Cedric mentioned, rubbing my feet. "I love you, Shugg."

"You're right. You are the luckiest man in the world. You have me!"

I leaned forward and kissed my baby. His lips were soft and full; just like they always were. We were sitting together inside Brown Sugar, waiting for Ramona to finally show up. She was usually early, but today, she decided to take her sweet ass time. Cedric didn't want me waiting alone, so he agreed to stay with me until she arrived. Since she was taking so long, he removed my shoes and began massaging my feet.

"Cocky, aren't we?"

"Not at all. I just know my worth. I think you know my worth too." I rubbed my stomach playfully. "You're a lucky man if I keep letting you put babies in me."

"Maybe you just like daddy's dick," he chuckled, leaning into me.

"That too."

We continued flirting like we didn't already have a baby and another on the way. Cedric's hand rose up to my calves and squeezed tightly.

"Umm," I moaned. "Right there. That feels good."

Ramona pushed the door to the boutique open. She had her granddaughter, Ari, with her, and a frustrated look on her face.

Ramona's timing couldn't have been worse. Her arrival stopped my pampering session.

"Shugg, sorry I'm late. That damn son of mine didn't show up this morning. I was waiting on him to pick up his daughter. That's why I'm late. I had to bring her with me. You know I hate being late!" Ramona removed her hat, allowing her brunette curls to fall loosely around her shoulders. They framed her pale face and chubby features.

"That's okay," I said with a smile. "You gotta do what you gotta do."

"That's true. I'm glad you understand, Shugg. Ari, go over there and sit down." Ramona pointed to a row of chairs next to Cedric and me. He slowly eased my feet off his lap and onto the floor.

"Well, it looks like y'all don't need me," Cedric mentioned, standing up. "I'll just be on my way."

He bent down and kissed me before smiling in Ramona's direction. She watched him exit and turned to me with a girlish grin.

"Shugg...I see why you stay pregnant. If I had all that up under me every night...Umm umm umm."

I turned toward Ari, who wasn't paying us any mind. She was focused intently on the large tablet in her hand. Combined with the earbuds in her ear, I doubted that she heard anything being said.

"You're too much, Ramona. What do you think your husband would say if he heard that?"

"As big as his eyes get when he sees these young hoes walking around here, he better not say nothing! Ain't nothing wrong with my eyes. I can look."

Ramona had a point. She could look all she wanted. I just needed for her to know that Cedric was all mine. He was off limits. Changing the subject, I got down to the matter at hand.

"So, you were very vague in what you were looking for. I believe you mentioned that you wanted a dress with three-quarter length sleeves. Black, right?"

"Oh yes! You know I love my black. It's the color that suits me best. You have a good memory, Shugg."

"In this business, you gotta have one." I walked to the front of the suite and grabbed my *iPad* sitting on top of the counter. I retrieved the notes I had made about her request. "Long, but not too long, form fitting, detailed in the back, comfortable, yet easy to take off if need be." Looking up from my device, I added, "Your words, not mine."

"You know how it is, Shugg. When you want it, you want it." She turned her attention to my stomach as she reached down and grabbed it. "Girl, you look like you're going to pop. How far along are you? Didn't you just have that handsome little boy?"

"Cree," I emphasized. "He's seven months. I still have another four months to go with my little girl."

"Girl!" Ramona clasped her hands together in excitement. "What a blessing. I wanted a little girl so bad, but after popping Jett out naturally, I closed up shop. Now that I have a granddaughter, I don't regret my decision. These kids and their damn attitudes."

"I hope you know I heard that," Ari said while rolling her neck.

I turned to Ramona to see what she was going to do next. I had no problem lending her one of the numerous belts hanging in my storage closest. Ari was too grown for her own good. Stephanie believed in letting the girl 'express herself.' As a result, she was disrespectful toward her elders.

"I don't give a damn if you did hear it," Ramona barked. "The truth is the truth. Kids now-a-days don't have respect. They don't have those old-school values that we used to have. Hell, I wouldn't have any teeth in my mouth if I talked to my mother the way you talk to me."

"So what? That's you."

It took everything in me to hold my composure. I had to tell myself that Ari wasn't mine and touching her could have my ass giving birth behind bars. Still, the little heifer needed to be addressed. If Ramona wasn't gonna do it, I sure as hell would.

"Just who do you think you're talking to?" Ramona huffed. "You must've lost your damn mind."

Ari rolled her eyes and blatantly ignored Ramona. It was something I saw Stephanie do when she didn't want to be bothered. Stephanie and Jett were responsible for the girl's rude behavior. I shook my head as Ramona's cheeks flushed in frustration.

Was this what I had to look forward to? An attitude was something I refused to deal with. If my daughter was anything like Ari, I would be doing some serious time. That girl needed her ass whooped.

DAVINA

"Girl...I don't know if I'm ready for a little girl. You should have seen Ari today! That little brat needed her ass beat."

"No, you didn't say 'beat,'" I chuckled. "Don't you mean, whooped?"

"No, I meant what I said. Beat! That girl is spoiled and talks to you like you ain't shit. I couldn't believe how Ari treated Ramona. That's her grandmother for God's sake."

"Ari? Ain't that Stephanie's daughter?" I questioned.

"Yeah, that's her. She came to the boutique with Ramona today. I guess Jett didn't show up to take her off Ramona's hands. Nobody knows where he's at."

"Probably somewhere fuckin' some hoe," I blurted out. *Damn*, I thought. *I didn't mean to say that out loud.* "I mean...maybe he just forgot."

"You meant what you said," Shugg snapped. "Don't try to change it now. Jett is Jett. He'll fuck anything with a pussy – including me."

"I didn't mean it like that, Shugg. I was talkin' about the *other* girls. You're not a hoe."

"And neither are the other women he's probably lyin' to. You know how slick Jett's mouth is."

"Whoa! Whoa! You're blowing this way out of proportion."

This wasn't the direction I thought our conversation would go. Initially, I was happy to see Shugg's number flash across my phone's screen. We usually talked several times a day; unless of course, we were *physically* in each other's presence. Shugg was my best friend, and besides my husband, she was the person I talked to the most. I had practically kidnapped her son and kept him overnight. I thought she would be calling to ask for him to return, but instead, she was giving me an attitude. Having her lash out at me for no reason at all wasn't the reaction I was seeking.

"What other way is it supposed to go, Davina? People are so quick to put the blame on the woman. Jett is responsible for his own actions. You can't blame me or any other woman who falls for his bullshit."

"No one is blaming you, Shugg!" I stood from my bed and tiptoed out of the room. My tone had increased a notch, and I didn't want to wake Cree. "What is wrong with you? Why are you so sensitive today? I made a comment that had *nothing* to do with you and you got all in your feelings. For what? This conversation has gone so far left, I don't think it can get right. You need to go to sleep and get your feelings in check. I'll talk to you later."

"What about my son?" Shugg asked.

"What about him? He's just fine right where he's at. He's sleeping. I'll bring him home when he wakes up. I'll call you when I'm on my way."

I had no intention of taking Cree home. Just because Shugg had a problem didn't mean that I had to cut my time with him short. That was her issue, and had nothing to do with Cree.

Genesis walked up behind me as I reentered my bedroom. I jumped as I felt his hands wrap around my waist.

"I'm sorry, baby," he whispered, pulling me close. "I didn't mean to scare you. You just looked so good; I couldn't resist."

"I look like shit, Genesis."

"Well, it's good shit...and I want it."

His hands found their way up the front of my shirt. He palmed my breasts and pushed his dick into my back. Any frustration that I had with Shugg was long gone. Having my dude around made everything else irrelevant.

"We can't. Cree is in there."

"But he's sleep," Genesis noted, kissing my neck softly.

"I know, but..."

"But nothing. Shugg and Cedric still get it in with a baby in the house. Why can't we?"

He grabbed my hand and pulled me into our guest bedroom. It had yet to be used, and we took our time christening every square inch of the space we could.

I allowed my husband to have me any way he wanted. We fucked both in the bed and on the chair, but when it came down to Genesis releasing his load, we somehow ended up on the floor. He tapped my side, signaling that his nut was rising. Instead of swallowing our kids, I allowed him to stay inside, and let his soldiers do what they do.

"Fuck!" he called out. His body was still shaking when he leaned over me. "Damn, that shit was good."

"I know," I responded confidently. "I know my pussy is good."

Genesis gave me a sly smile before crawling to his feet. I laid there, enjoying the relaxed state that my body was in, while he exited and retreated to the shower. Normally, I would have joined him. The shower was usually the site for round two and maybe three, if I was lucky, but my mind was somewhere else. I laid there thinking about what it would be like if Genesis and I had a child of our own. I had a great day with Cree, and to be honest, I didn't want him to go home. Kids weren't something I thought about having, but both Cree and Genesis were wearing me down.

Genesis peeked his head into the room after his shower. I was still on my back on the floor, staring up at the ceiling. My legs were in the air with my feet pointed toward the ceiling.

"What the hell?" Genesis chuckled. "What the hell are you doing, Davina?"

"I'm guiding the sperm to the egg."

"You're what?" Genesis turned his nose up in confusion and slowly walked toward me.

"I saw it in a movie once," I explained. "If you hold your legs up, it's supposed to help the sperm migrate to the right place."

"That's crazy." He shook his head and knelt down next to me.

I started to put my legs down, but he stopped me. "You better put them legs back up! If this crazy shit is gonna get me a son, you can keep your legs up all night!"

"What if it's a girl?"

He thought about it. "On second thought, put them legs down. We can try again later."

I pushed his arm playfully. "Whatever!"

BLISS

"Do you like this dress?" Stephanie asked me.

I glanced in her direction and turned my nose up. "No. That's ugly."

She placed the 80's style dress back on the rack and continued searching. I didn't take her as a 'rack' person. As much money as she had, I assumed that she would be buying something designer or having something specifically made for the occasion. It was just an assumption. I really didn't know her like that.

"It's so hard to find something," Stephanie huffed. She placed her hand on her hip and pushed her hair out of her face. "This is what I get for waiting until the last minute."

She was right. Steele and Nessa were renewing their vows tomorrow. My shit had been together for weeks. I was surprised when she called and asked if I would ride with her to pick something out. Ty and our son were straight as well, but I decided to roll with Stephanie to look at possible accessories.

She showed out by picking me up in her late model Maserati. It was cute; I'll give her that, but it was way too sporty to be driven to a *basic* strip mall. We weren't even on the good side of town. If she knew what I knew, she would be cautious of where she parked her ride. Since she wasn't worried about it, I wasn't either. We window shopped at a few places before going into one of the stores. It was trendy, but the rack that caught Stephanie's eye probably would have appealed more to my great grandmother. The items were hideous!

"What about this one?" Stephanie pulled a sequined dress from the rack and held it up to her body.

"Are you going to a wedding or a Disco Ball?"

She rolled her eyes and put the dress back. "Thanks a lot, Bliss. I thought you were here to help."

"I'm trying to help, but you can't be serious. Stephanie...Look at you. You have a nice body. Almost anything would look good on you. Why do you keep choosing these 'grandma' outfits? They're horrible."

"I think they're cute," Stephanie added, with an attitude. "I like different. I don't like looking like everyone else."

"They're not different, Stephanie. They're ugly!"

"Well, what would you suggest?" she challenged.

I laughed it off and walked toward the other side of the boutique. "I never said fashion was my forte. I just know what I like. Shugg... now, she can get you together!" I turned around just as Stephanie rolled her eyes. "What's all that for?"

"I won't be taking any advice from Shugg."

"Why not?" I asked, cocking my head to the side.

"Really, Bliss? Everybody knows our issue."

"True, but why is it still a problem? You've both moved on. You're not even married to the guy anymore. The issue should be squashed."

"That's easy for you to say. Everyone speaks so highly of the girl, and all I can think about is her fucking my husband."

"Your *ex-husband*," I corrected, "stepped out on his marriage. That has nothing to do with Shugg. She didn't owe you any loyalty. *He* did."

"You just don't get it."

"Oh, I get it. It's just not what you want to hear." I located a rack with stylish dresses more appropriate for the twenty-first century. I began rummaging through the selections while explaining to

Stephanie where I was coming from. "Let me ask you this...what would you say if I told you Emory was married?"

"He's not married," Stephanie stated, laughing off my question.

"I know he's not, but what if he was. You two have had sex, right?"

"I'm not telling you that!"

"Ok, that's a 'yes.' Back to my question...knowing you've already slept with him, if I told you he was married, what would you say?"

"What could I say? The damage would have already been done."

"True, but how would you feel if I started calling you a home-wrecker?"

"How would I be a homewrecker if you just told me he was married?" It took a few seconds for the realization to set in, but when it did, she got the point.

"I'm not trying to open any old wounds. You kicked that loser to the curb, but you can't be mad at Shugg forever. It's not like she kept doing it. Once she found out the truth, she cut off all ties. He lied to both of y'all. That's not her fault, Stephanie."

"I guess you're right. It's just...I don't know."

"You gotta let that hurt go. You're mad at the wrong person." A cream-colored dress caught my eye. It was simple and shape-hugging, but with the right accessories, Stephanie could easily pull it off. "What do you think about this?"

Stephanie gave the dress a once over before her eyes lit up with excitement. "I love it!"

"Good. Let's go." I handed the dress to Stephanie and began walking toward the front of the store.

"Wait! We're only going to look at one dress? What if I like something else?"

Rolling my eyes, I returned to the rack and browsed through the rest of the garments. I was starting to develop an attitude. I should have ignored her call.

"You've been with Ty for a while, right?" Stephanie pressed, revisiting our conversation.

"Yeah, why?"

"Well then, you should at least understand where I'm coming

from. I don't hate Shugg. I know Jett lied to her. He lied to both of us, but imagine if you were in my shoes. Every time you came around your new man's family, you have to see the face of the woman who slept with your ex. Even if she wasn't at fault, it's still hard. That's all I'm saying. It's going to take some time."

"I understand that. You don't have to be best friends with the girl...Just smile and keep it cute."

After she broke it down, I guess I *did* understand her point of view. I wouldn't want to see the person who fucked my ex either. Thankfully, that wasn't something I had to deal with. That was her problem, not mine.

STEPHANIE

Shugg was the last person I wanted to talk about. Everyone could praise her all they wanted to, but for me...I needed time. That *time*, didn't include spending my day discussing one of my ex's mistresses.

After nothing else on the rack caught my eye, I moved on to a different section of the boutique. I ended up going with the crème dress Bliss picked out, with a wide leather belt to accent my waist.

"Are you hungry?" I questioned, as we walked back toward the car.

"Not really. I need to get back to my baby. I want to take him to the park while it's still light outside."

I got the vibe that she was lying, but at that particular moment, I really didn't care. Our presence together had been awkward after telling Bliss how I felt. Her brother was married to Davina, and Davina was best friends with Shugg. I understood it. She knew Shugg longer, and her loyalty was to her. I just wasn't going to sit back and let someone else tell me how I should feel.

"No problem. I need to drop some things off to Ari anyway."

I drove Bliss back to her place and dropped her off. We agreed to get together after the ceremony, but to be honest, I agreed just to send her on her way. If we got together, we got together. It wasn't that big of a deal to me.

I went to my house and showered before dealing with Ari and her father. It just so happened that the shoes she wanted to wear with her new sundress were left at home. Instead of forcing her to wear what she had, or buying a suitable alternative, Jett had Ari called me. She cried for three minutes straight until I gave in and agreed to bring the shoes to her. I had just enough time to get a quick nap before driving over half an hour to Ramona's house. That's what intended to do, but as soon as my head hit the pillow, Jett called changing my plans completely.

"Hello," I answered, rolling over in the bed.

"Steph?"

"Yeah, it's me. Is everything alright with Ari?"

"She's fine. My mom has her for a while." He paused momentarily to clear his throat. "How are you doing?"

"I'm good."

"You sound good."

I rolled my eyes and huffed. "What do you want, Jett? I'm tired and in the bed."

"Good thing I called," he responded enthusiastically. "I just so happen to be in the area. I can swing by and get Ari's shoes if you want. It'll save you a trip."

"Just so happened my ass. What are you up to?"

"Nothing."

"Can I come by or what?"

"I'll have them ready for you."

I laid in the bed until I heard the chime of my ringing doorbell. Wrapping a robe around my half-dressed body, I opened it to a bouquet of red roses partially hiding Jett's face. He extended them in my direction and flashed a million-dollar smile.

"These are for you."

"You shouldn't have, Jett. Really...you shouldn't have."

"But I did. Will you at least take them?"

Taking the flowers from his hand, I stepped back allowing him to enter. He took his time brushing past me. I sighed loudly, letting him know I wasn't dealing with any of his shit.

"Wait right here," I instructed, pointing toward my living room. "I'll be right back."

I threw the flowers on my leather chaise and proceeded up the stairs to Ari's room. I opened her closed closet and was surprised with the pigsty I found. I searched through the mountain of shoes Ari had thrown in the back of her closet. The sight alone had me ready to get on my hands and knees and sort the pile out myself. I hated a dirty house. Even though the closet wasn't technically dirty, it was in need of a good straightening up. I made a mental note to discuss it with Ari when she returned home in a few days.

When I traveled back down the stairs, I noticed Jett making himself comfortable. He removed his loafers and untucked his button-down from his slacks.

"What do you think you're doing?" I asked, descending the last step. "You can put your shoes right back on."

"Come on now, Steph. It's been a long day. Can I just chill for a minute?"

"You can chill all you want...at your momma's house!"

My words were meant to hurt. After doing me wrong, and stepping out on our marriage, he took his bags and moved back in with his mother. After all, it was my dime supporting our extravagant lifestyle. I was born into money and my ex benefited greatly. Unfortunately for him, he didn't think about the consequences of his actions. Jett entered our marriage with the clothes on his back and in our divorce, he left with the same thing he came with.

He stood to his feet and tried to use his charm to make me change my mind. "You don't miss me, Steph? 'Cause I damn sure miss the hell outta you."

"No, I don't," I told him, throwing the shoes in his direction. He caught them with his quick reflexes. "I don't miss you at all."

The doorbell rang again as Jett stepped toward me. It was perfect timing, getting me out of an awkward situation. As I opened the door without confirming the person on the other side, Emory's face appeared, making the situation even more uncomfortable than it once was.

"Emory!" I called out in surprise. "What are you doing here?"

"I stopped by to see my lady." He kissed me on the cheek and entered my place without an invitation. When he saw Jett, he smirked and pulled me close. "Am I interrupting something?"

"No, he was just leaving," I advised, pleading with my eyes for Jett to just take the shoes and leave. Instead, he stood tall like he was really about something.

"Yeah, you're interrupting something alright," Jett began, clearing his throat. "I need to talk to my wife...in private."

"Jett, stop. I'm not your wife," I huffed, rolling my eyes. "You have what you came for, now go."

"We're not done talking. I meant what I said, Steph."

If he wanted a reaction from Emory, he didn't get one. Just as cool as can be, Emory pulled me closer, kissed me on the lips, and gripped the back of my ass tightly.

"Finish talking to the clown," he advised. "I'll be in the room when you're done." With a wink, he added, "You know I don't like to wait."

Jett's mouth was still open as Emory disappeared up the stairs. Jett might have talked a good game, but Emory was a problem he didn't want.

"You're really choosing him over me," Jett whispered, careful to not let Emory hear his words. "Steph, we can work this out. I'm ready."

"The time for working things out passed a long time ago. You should have thought about that while we were married."

I walked toward the door and held it open for him. Accepting defeat, he slowly strolled over to me, and pleaded his case one last time.

"Steph, I'm sorry. Truly, I am. I've changed. Let me show you."

"The only thing I want to see, is you walking back to your car." Adding insult to injury, I untied my belt, let my robe fall open, and tied it back again. His eyes widened at the tease of the lace bra and panty set underneath. "Now go. I don't want to keep my man waiting."

He stepped out the door with both pairs of shoes in his hand. He opened his mouth to speak, but I closed the door in his face. I had business to handle.

NESSA

I broke down. The weight of everything going on was just too much to bear. I was past my breaking point, and I couldn't stop the tears from flowing down my face even if I wanted to. I stood in the parking lot of Head Bangerz preparing to go in, when Steele appeared in the doorway. He looked around cautiously before stepping out. Once outside, he dialed a number on his cell and brought his phone to his ear. Steele paced the front of the building while smiling from ear to ear. I didn't know who was on the other end, but whoever it was put a smile on his face.

At one time, that person used to be me. Steele and I were inseparable. I felt honored just being in his presence. He could have had any woman he wanted, yet he chose me. Me! I didn't deserve him, nor was I on his level. We came from two different worlds, and if it wasn't for meeting in school, our paths probably would have never crossed.

I leaned against my car to remain hidden. Steele couldn't see me, but I sure as hell could see him. I was parked in the middle of the crowded parking lot and had a bird's eye view of my husband. After his phone call, he waited around as if he was expecting someone. When a late model car pulled up and a tall, beautiful woman exited, he immediately walked over to greet her. It was apparent that Steele was waiting for the woman, and when he took her hand and led her into the building, my floodgates opened even more.

He treated me like a queen just the day before. Not only did he add some new ice to my finger, he wined and dined me, and treated me to a mini shopping spree. He had me rethinking my whole plan. Maybe, just maybe, I was giving up too soon. I thought he was coming around. That was my own stupidity.

I reached for my door handle, but a soft hand stopped me. I turned around to see Chandra behind me. I didn't know how long Steele's mother had been standing there.

"Where are you going?" she asked in a stern tone.

Wiping my face, I sniffed back a fresh set of tears threatening to fall. "Home."

She took a step toward me and shook her head. "You better grow a damn backbone. I know you saw the same thing I did. That was my son, right?"

I nodded.

"So, you mean to tell me that your husband walked in there with another woman and you're going home? You don't see a problem with that?"

"Chandra, I-"

"Don't 'Chandra' me. You've been my daughter for too long to start being formal now. It's always been 'Mom.' What's different now?"

She was right. I did look at her as a mother figure. My own mother wasn't worth shit and Chandra was the next best thing. She had been nothing but good to me. Chandra treated me just like she treated everyone else; tough, but fair.

"Mom, I just...Steele is...my heart just can't take this anymore."

The tears streamed down my face. I wiped them away with Chandra looking on. She didn't sugarcoat shit. She wasn't fazed by my somber attitude. After I stopped sniffling and crying, she got me together.

"Are you done?" she asked with a straight face. "Because all that crying shit can stop. Look at you...fuckin' up your makeup and shit."

"You don't understand, Mom. You don't know what I've been going through."

"You *do* know who you're talking to, right? I'm a St. John, just like you. The only difference is, I ain't gonna sit back and take that shit. That man is *your* husband. You gotta be smart. Like I said, he just walked in there with another woman. What are *you* gonna do?"

Her words gave me a newfound confidence. I stood up straight and squared my shoulders. I combed my fingers through my hair and sucked my teeth. I was gonna do something about it.

"I'm going in there," I stated matter-of-factly.

"Good! Claim what's yours. That's *your* man. You took vows with him. Don't let him disrespect you like that. Walk right up in there in and put him in his place. I'll go with you."

With Chandra by my side, I had the courage of ten men. I strutted my stuff in a fitted black jumpsuit and wedge heels. I didn't dress specifically for the club. I just wanted to feel pretty and enjoy a night on the town; even if it wasn't with my husband. I set out to catch a movie or something, but my curiosity led me to Head Bangerz. Steele said he would be there, and I stopped by to spy on him. I saw enough to make me turn around to rethink my reasoning for coming there in the first place, but Chandra was determined to make me stand my ground.

I walked in and headed straight to the basement. That's where the offices were located, and just like I thought, Steele was down there chopping it up with the same female he walked in with. She was sitting on the edge of his desk while he stood in front of her. I opened the door and walked straight in.

"What's going on here?" I asked, stepping in between them. Chandra stood in the doorway and watched me work.

"Nessa!" Steele said, taking a step back from the woman. "Hey. What are you doing here?"

"Do I have to have a reason to stop by and see my husband?"

The chick cocked her neck to the side in confusion. "Husband? Steele, you have a wife? You never told me you were married."

Chandra cleared her throat. I picked up on what she was trying to do. I turned to the girl, and asked, "Would that *really* have made a difference? Come on now; I know the game. I wasn't born yesterday."

"Ba-ba-baby," Steele stuttered. "It's not what it looks like. She's just..."

"She's what?" I cut him off. "One of the numerous hoes you're fuckin'? Who is she, Steele?"

"I think I should go." The woman eased off the desk and slow strutted toward the door. She was careful not to take her eyes off me. I was liable to swing on the bitch; just off GP.

"Destiny, that's probably best," Steele stated weakly. "We'll link up tomorrow."

"Destiny, is it?" I repeated. "Steele won't be linking up with you tomorrow or any other day. I don't know what he told you, but it's not that type of party. You can go."

Destiny paused before turning to Steele. If she wanted him to say something, she would be waiting for a while. Steele stood there with his mouth open, surprised at my boldness. Out of the corner of my eye, I noticed Chandra smiling in satisfaction.

"Did you hear what I said? You can leave, or if you want, I can make you leave. Either way is fine with me."

"Steele?!" Destiny pleaded. "Say something."

"His wife said it for him," Chandra interjected. "If you knew what was good for you, you'd get out of here while you still have the chance."

Destiny huffed in frustration and stomped out of the office. Chandra closed the door and followed her. I'm sure Steele's mother had a few choice words for the girl, but I was more concerned with the man standing in front of me.

"Nessa, what the fuck is this all about? What are you doing here? Man...you brought my mom into this bullshit. This shit is crazy..."

"Shut up!" I yelled. He froze at my audacity. Walking up to him, I took full advantage of the situation. "You shut the hell up and listen. If I catch another bitch up in here with you, I'll clean our account out so fast; you won't even have a pot to piss in. Do you understand me?"

"I'm listening," he mouthed through gritted teeth. A thick vein in his forehead bulged in frustration.

"Good." I took a deep breath. "Happy wife, happy life... Remember that." I patted his cheek and smiled. "See you tomorrow."

"Nessa!" he called out as I stepped away from him. "Nessa! We're not done talking."

"Oh, yes, we are. The conversation ends when I say so."

5

FEBRUARY 14TH

SHUGG

I had to give it to Nessa. She went all out for the vow renewal ceremony. The church was decorated in various shades of pink; accented by huge floral centerpieces up and down the aisleway. Cedric and I silently took our seats as the crowd slowly began to pile in.

"Steele came off some serious doe with all this," Cedric stated, sitting down beside me. Although we had assigned seats, he allowed me to take the aisle, so I could stretch out if need be.

"I know. It's beautiful."

"And expensive."

I tapped Cedric playfully on the arm as he pointed out the obvious. It was expensive all right, but according to Davina, Steele could more than afford it.

Silently, I surveyed the large room. The sanctuary had been transformed into something straight out of a movie. The pews had way too many bows, sashes, and ribbons to count. The over-the-top decorations didn't stop there. Each person was given a program with pages and pages of color photos highlighting milestones over the years. I began flipping through the small booklet when Cedric stood from his seat and greeted the couple walking toward us. It was Stephanie and Emory.

"Hey," Cedric said, extending his hand. "Shouldn't you be back there with the groomsmen?"

"Yeah, I'm about to head that way. I wanted to make sure Stephanie made it to her seat first."

"It's good to see you again, Stephanie," Cedric greeted with a smile. "You look beautiful as always."

"Alright now," Emory teased. "Don't be pushing up on my woman."

Stephanie playfully tapped him on the chest. "Oh, Emory, hush. You know he's not pushing up on me. He got Shugg for that." She gave me a wink and flashed a fake smile. "Shugg, you're glowing."

"Thank you," I mouthed, turning away from her.

Cedric felt the tension mounting between us and intervened. "How's Steele doing? Is he ready to say, 'I do' twice?"

"Man..." Emory said with a chuckle. "I sure hope so. It would a be a shame if they spent all this money for nothing. Naw, I'm just playing. Steele's ready. He loves that girl. They're gonna be together forever."

"Well," Stephanie interrupted. "It was nice seeing you two. Emory, baby, it's almost that time. I need to get to my seat."

Cedric slowly eased back down beside me as the pair retreated to the other side of the sanctuary. I wondered if my girl, Davina had anything to do with us sitting on opposite sides. Stephanie's attitude toward me was getting under my skin. The more distance between us, the better.

A soft melody played as more people entered and took their seats. When Davina peeked her head through the door and motioned for me to follow, I handed Cedric both my purse and program and stood to my feet.

"Hold this. I'll be right back."

"Wait. Where are you going?" he asked as I started down the aisle. I didn't answer him. Instead, I continued on until I caught up with my friend.

She pulled me toward a corner. That's when I got a good look at her smeared makeup distraught face.

"Davina, what's wrong?"

"Everything," she huffed. "Everything is wrong. I can't do this, Shugg. I thought I could, but I can't."

"You're overacting," I chuckled. "Davina, you're a bridesmaid. All you have to do is stand there and smile. That's not hard for you to do."

Whatever I said caused Davina to cry uncontrollably. I tried to console her as best as I could; careful to prevent her tears from spilling onto her rose-colored dress.

"Davina, relax. You'll do just fine."

"No, I won't. I'm not ready. I need more time."

"Not ready? What are you talking about? Girl, what's wrong? This isn't like you."

"I'm pregnant," she finally revealed through sniffles. "I've had a feeling for a while. I just didn't want to believe it. I finally got the nerve to take a test today. I just had to know. It was positive."

"Davina!" I shouted. "That's great news! Genesis is gonna be so happy!"

Nervously, she glanced around before putting her index finger to her lips. "Will you keep it down? I haven't told him yet."

"Why not?"

"Because," she snapped. "I was cool when we were talking about it, but now it's real. This is terrible."

"No, it's not. That man has been wanting a baby, and now he's about to have one. You need to accept what is and embrace it." I grabbed for her stomach and she swatted my hand away. "Davina's having a baby," I cooed. "I'm happy for you, girl."

"I'm not happy. I'm terrified."

"That's because it's still new. Give it some time; you'll come around. In the meantime, tell your husband the good news, before I do."

"You better not," she warned.

"Well, then...make sure you do it. Make that man's day, girl. He's going to be so excited!" I straightened her off-the-shoulder dress and smoothed a stray hair that had fell in her face. "Come on. Let's go get your makeup fixed. We don't need everyone asking you what's wrong."

Davina led me up the stairs, to a large room. Women were scrambling around getting their last-minute details in order. Bliss chased her young son around while two women, who I didn't know, took turns zipping each other's dresses. Another woman sat in a makeup chair, but quickly stood when she saw the disaster that had become of Davina's makeup.

"Ooo, Davina. Look at you. You need this chair more than me. Zelda!" she called out. "We need you to work your magic."

I told Davina I would see her downstairs. She smiled as Zelda the make-up artist, shimmied back over with her make-up bag in hand. I took the time to step toward Nessa and compliment her choice of dress.

"Aye, girl, you single?" I teased.

She smiled and stepped toward me. "Shugg, you're so silly. Thanks for coming."

"Thanks for inviting me. You look absolutely beautiful. That dress is gorgeous on you. Steele is gonna flip when he sees you."

"I hope so. I can't believe I'm really doing this again. I wanted to do something grand for our anniversary, but now, I'm not so sure."

"It's just your nerves. That's normal. It'll all be over soon, and you'll be off on your second honeymoon." I leaned in closer and added, "Lucky you."

That brought a smile to her face. She rubbed her hands together and I almost went blind.

"That ring! Is it new?"

"Oh, this?" She wiggled her fingers in front of me and smiled. "Yeah, Steele proposed...again."

The whole carat I was rocking wasn't even comparable. Steele went all out for Nessa.

"Maybe Steele should give Cedric a few pointers. He definitely has good taste."

"Girl, stop! Your ring is beautiful. And when you walk down the aisle, Cedric is gonna hook you up with something even better. Watch and see."

"If it ever happens. Until Cedric stops putting these kids in me, I ain't walking nowhere. I refuse to look like a whale on my wedding day."

"You gotta start saying no, girl."

"But it feels so good."

Stephanie tapped me on the arm. Together we laughed and enjoyed the moment.

DAVINA

"Out!" Bliss demanded, pushing Genesis out the door. "No men allowed!"

"Come on, Bliss. I gotta talk to my wife about something." Genesis muscled his way in the room, lifting his hands to cover his eyes. "I don't see nothing," he declared.

"Genesis, you know better!" Nessa huffed. "Did Steele send you in here?"

"He doesn't even know I'm here. I need to talk to Davina."

I stood from my seat, pulling Genesis by the arm. We stepped out of the room and into the long hallway.

"What?" I asked after closing the door.

"I missed you."

He leaned in to kiss me, warming my insides. It was hard to be mad when he was so sweet. Genesis did things just to make me smile. He was different from every other man that I had ever dated. He was truly the love of my life and I was honored to be his wife.

"I just saw you," I mentioned, leaning my head back as his kisses trailed down my neck.

"You know I don't like being away from you for a long time," he said in between kisses. "Somebody might be trying to take what's mine."

Bliss emerged from the dressing room and glanced down both sides of the hall. Catching us in action, she turned her nose up and shook her head.

"This is a church for crying out loud! Get a room!"

Genesis kissed me one last time before stepping back. "Don't be mad 'cause Ty ain't doing the same thing to you."

Bliss rolled her eyes. "Whatever. Where is Ty, by the way? I need him to get the baby. He's in here acting a fool."

"He was in there talking to Steele last time I saw him."

"This is the shit I'm talking about," Bliss complained. "He knows I have things to do. He should have already had the baby."

"Sis, this is a church for crying out loud," Genesis stated, throwing her words back at her. "No cussing in the Lord's house."

Bliss gave him the finger and rolled her eyes.

"God saw that I hope you know," Genesis added with a chuckle. "Go get my nephew. I'll take him to his daddy. I'm headed that way anyway."

"Thank you." Bliss returned to the room and retrieved her son. She reappeared with a firm hold on her son's hand and his bag thrown across her shoulder. "And tell Ty we need to talk after the ceremony."

"Will do. Come on, lil' man." Genesis started down the hall until he realized I wasn't following behind. "You too. Bring your fine ass on."

I followed Genesis down the hall and up another flight of stairs. There was another large room off the stairs, which dubbed as the men's dressing room. Genesis opened the door, and I heard men gossiping like females.

"You see this shit?" Steele asked with widened eyes. He passed his phone to his brother, Emory. "Shorty is thick as hell."

"Damn," Emory responded, biting down on his closed fist. "I'm 'bout to start following that broad on Instagram. What's her name?"

Ty jumped up from his seat to get a good look, along with the other men who were a part of the groom's party. Everyone couldn't get enough of whatever girl had their attention. They acted as though they had never seen tits and ass before. Well, that's what I'm assuming it was. I didn't see the picture for myself.

Genesis cleared his throat, bringing attention to our trio in the doorway.

"Really, bro," Steele smirked, taking possession of his phone once again. "You brought a woman into the man cave. You got her spying on us?"

"Ain't nobody spying on you," I said, stepping into the room. "Blame your brother. It wasn't my idea to come down here."

Ty held his hands out from his son and the boy ran to his father. Genesis handed him his son's bag and cut his eyes at Steele.

"My wife can go anywhere she wants to. Ain't that right, baby?"

He looked at me for confirmation, but I didn't have anything for him. Instead, I made my rounds, giving the well-dressed men both hugs and compliments.

"You clean up well, Steele," I said, readjusting his tie. "Nessa's a lucky woman."

"Davina, I knew you wanted me," he replied with a wink. "You're cool and all, but my baby bro is selfish. He doesn't like to share."

"Damn right!" Genesis' voice boomed behind me. "When you got something good, you wanna keep it to yourself." His lips found my neck again, and he pecked softly.

"Man, go on with all that!" Steele complained. "We gotta finish getting ready."

Before I knew it, bottles were being popped and passed around. I looked down to see a glass of brown liquor being handed in my direction.

"You're really about to drink in a church?" I asked Genesis as he brought his glass to his lips.

"Damn right. It's just to take the edge off. Nothing serious. It's not like I'm about to get drunk. Drink up." He took his drink to the head and glanced over at me. "What are you waiting for?"

"I don't want it," I lied, trying to get out of it. I attempted to pass the drink back to Genesis, but he wouldn't take it.

"It's just one drink. What's the problem?"

Our exchange caught the attention of everyone else in the room. Steele started a chant and got everyone else into it as well.

"Drink it! Drink it! Drink it!"

Even the baby sat his too grown ass up and started repeating what he heard everyone else saying. As a pregnant woman, drinking was something I wasn't going to do.

"Will y'all just leave me alone?! It's not that serious. It's liquor."

"Quit talking and get to it," Emory added with a smirk. "What are you waiting for? Drink up, baby girl. It'll make you feel better."

"I can't," I replied, barely audible.

"Why not?" Genesis questioned, eyeing me skeptically.

I leaned in and whispered in his ear. "Because I'm pregnant."

A wide smile formed on his face and he leaned back and searched for truth in my eyes.

"You for real?"

I nodded.

"Aye! I'm gonna be a daddy y'all!" Genesis announced. "My swimmers did their thing! Davina's pregnant."

"Congrats, bro," Steele mentioned, giving his brother some dap. "That's what's up!"

Emory stepped toward me and snatched the glass from my hand. "You're pregnant, girl. What do you think you're doing? You ain't supposed to be drinking."

No shit, I thought.

BLISS

"Bliss!" my mother called out.

"Yes," I responded, dreading what she had to say. I stuck my head in the sanctuary for two seconds and she managed to sneak up behind me.

"What's the holdup? The service was supposed to start fifteen minutes ago. Everyone is waiting."

"That's what I came down here to find out. No one can find Steele or Nessa."

"This is ridiculous! How can you lose both the bride *and* groom?"

That's what I wanted to know. I had been looking for Nessa, while Genesis and Emory were out looking for Steele. Being that no one could find them, I assumed they were together.

"I don't know, Mom. I'll keep looking."

I strolled off in the opposite direction, but she followed behind barking orders to everyone she encountered.

"Hey...you?" she asked a man dressed in a waiter uniform. "Have you seen my son?"

The Hispanic man stared at her in confusion before smiling shyly. He looked her up and down before folding his hands in front of him.

"Do you hear me talking to you? I said...have you seen my son? Steele?"

"Mom," I said with a sigh. "I don't think he understands you."

"Of course, he understands me. What's not to understand?" She turned her attention back to the man and asked, "You do know who my son is, right? The groom. The man that's getting married."

Once again, the man stared at her as though he hadn't heard a word she said. Seeing the frustration on my mother's face, I intervened.

"Do you speak English?" I quizzed. He didn't respond. "Do you speak Spanish?"

"Espanol?"

"Yeah, that."

He went off rolling his tongue and speaking his native language, giving my mother her answer. Like I told her before, he didn't understand what she was saying. In true Chandra fashion, my mother told him to get back to work and followed me up the hall. She had to feel superior, no matter what the situation was.

"When I find that boy," my mother began behind me, "I'm gonna ring his neck! He knows better. He got all those people waiting. Some of them have traveled a long way just to see this ceremony. It's selfish...of both of them."

"Let's find out where they're at first, Mom. Maybe something is going on. We don't want to jump to conclusions."

"Bliss, think about who you're talking about. Steele ain't in danger. That boy has one thing on his mind, and if I took a wild guess, I'd say they're in one of these rooms somewhere."

I put two and two together and realized what she was talking about. "No," I declared. "Not in a church."

"He's your father's child," she replied simply. "That boy is nasty with a capital 'N'."

I chuckled as I started up a flight of stairs. The back of my feet weren't doing me any justice as they began aching in my stiletto heels. The dress Nessa chose for me was pretty, but it was made to be seen and not worn. It hugged my body tightly, leaving no room for me to move around. Going up the steps proved to be more of a challenge than it was worth. If my mother wasn't following behind, I would hid somewhere, and pretended to be looking.

"We better find them fast," my mother warned. "I'm not walking all around this church. I'ma give it one more go-round, then I'm going right back down these stairs and sending everyone home."

"You can't do that, Mom."

"Watch me! They should be ashamed of themselves. They have people worried sick and they're out doing whatever."

By the time I got to the top of the stairs, I was winded and out of breath. I took a few seconds to regain my composure before starting down the hall. I ran into two other members of the wedding party, but they couldn't provide any information. I gave up my quest once my mother started with her mouth once again. I loved my mother, but her mouth was something I just didn't want to deal with.

"I'm going back to the sanctuary," I announced. "When Steele and Nessa decide to show their faces, I'll be waiting."

"Bliss!" my mother called out behind me. "Get back here!"

That was the last thing I was going to do. I was hot, grouchy, and over it! I came to see a wedding; not play hide and seek with the bride and groom.

"I ain't got time for it," I called over my shoulder. I removed my shoes and walked back down the stairs barefoot.

Ty was fixing his suit jacket when I stepped back in the sanctuary. As soon as I caught up to him, I got in his ass.

"Where's our son?"

"He's with Davina," Ty said simply. "I've been ripping and running looking for Steele. He wanted to go. Besides, she needs the practice."

"Why would she need practice with our son?" I asked, placing my hand on my hip.

"You must not have heard the news. She's pregnant."

"What? Davina's pregnant?" I couldn't help the surprise in my voice. As much as my sister-in-law claimed she didn't want any kids, it was hard to believe that she was expecting.

"Yeah. You should see Genesis. He's happy as hell."

I was happy for my brother. He had a big heart and would be a great dad. He was my son's favorite uncle, and soon, he would have a child of his own – a biological child.

"Where's he at? I need to congratulate him."

"Out looking for Steele."

"Maybe he'll have more luck than I did. I don't know where they are."

"You can only do what you can do. We tried." He turned me around and brought his hands to my shoulders. Slowly, he began to massage them.

"We did all we can do."

I peered over my shoulder at the handsome man behind me. Ty was everything that I wanted and more. I didn't deserve him. The skeletons I had in my closet were enough to make him leave, as long as they stayed hidden, I was good.

"I'm tired. They're grown. I'm staying out of their business. The only thing I'm worried about right now is my son, my man, and my own happiness."

"And another baby?" he asked, pausing my massage.

"You been drinking?" I teased.

"Just a little bit, but I'm serious. Why not? You and Davina can be pregnant at the same time."

"You had more than you think you had," I acknowledged, smelling the liquor on his breath.

"I ain't drunk, though. This is how I see it...We've been together all this time. I know I ain't going nowhere. You're the only one I want to have kids with."

"You give me a ring; I'll give you another baby," I challenged, knowing my demand would end the conversation.

I didn't expect him to agree to it. Ty told me from jump, that marriage wasn't something he wanted. Instead of laughing in my face, he fucked me all the way up.

"Deal."

STEPHANIE

The whole place was in disarray. The pretty decorations and beautiful arrangements were overshadowed by the loud conversations taking place. The church had been transformed into a makeshift meeting spot. People were talking amongst themselves, kids were running around, and I could have sworn I saw the pastor pull a steel flask from under his robe.

I sat quietly off to the side. I felt like the red-headed stepchild who didn't belong. Emory was MIA; apparently along with Nessa and Steele. Unlike everyone else in attendance, I could have cared less if Nessa and Steele walked down the aisle again or not. Hell, they were already married. It wasn't like anything was going to change. I wanted the day to be over – and quick.

"I'm gonna have to teach my son some manners?" Emory's father said with a chuckle. He took a sip from the glass in his hand and gulped it down quickly. "You never leave your woman unattended. Especially if she's as beautiful as you."

I blushed as he lowered himself down next to me. Genesis Sr was quite a gentleman. His compliments flowed effortlessly, making anyone in his presence feel special. His voice commanded attention.

It didn't hurt that he was easy on the eye. He was just as handsome as all four of his sons, and he knew it.

"Mind if I sit down?" he asked after he already planted his behind in the seat.

"Sure. Why not? It's not like anybody's breaking their neck to talk to me anyway."

"You gotta network. You can't expect everyone to come to you. We ain't that kinda family." He took another gulp of his drink and continued. "If you ain't the outgoing type, just give it time. That's all I can say. My kids are just like me. We're selective with who we fuck with. Excuse my language. We rock with who we know."

"It's cool," I mouthed, wanting him to continue. "What do you suggest I do?" Although I was getting closer with Emory, I couldn't say the same for me and his family. They tolerated me because they loved him. That much was obvious.

"Sitting by yourself, not talking to nobody isn't going to get people to talk to you. Get up, interact, mingle a little bit; hell, have a drink."

He passed the remaining contents of his cup in my direction, but I respectfully declined. Emory's father was a known ladies' man, and my mouth wasn't following behind his.

"Suit yourself, but if you wanna fit in, you're gonna have to lighten up. Emory ain't gonna always be around. You gotta learn how to hold your own." Glancing up, he spotted Shugg and Davina, and hurriedly stepped to his feet. "Davina! What's the holdup? Where's Steele? Let's get this show on the road. I got places to be."

"Dad, I was gonna ask you the same thing. I don't know what's going on. Genesis and I just left the guys. They were upstairs getting dressed."

"Apparently, no one can find either one of them. I thought they just stepped aside for a minute and you know...get a quickie in. Now I'm starting to get worried. Where's Nessa's sister? Does she know where they are?"

"Who Leesey? She just took all the kids downstairs. If she knows something, she sure didn't say anything to me." A distraught look crossed his face and Davina tried her best to ease it. "I'm sure they're fine, Dad. Let's go find Genesis. They're probably all together." Davina grabbed his hand and pulled him in the opposite direction. Over her shoulder she yelled, "Stay right there, Shugg. I'll be right back."

We shared an awkward glance. Shugg didn't want to be next to me just as much as I didn't want her to be. Instead of getting an attitude, and acting a damn fool, I decided to keep it cordial.

"Hello, again," I mouthed.

Shugg gave me a long, bored look. She wasn't feeling my sad attempt at a conversation. "Hi."

I was surprised when she sat down beside me and pulled out her phone. I glanced over to see her ultrasound picture as her screen-saver. I remembered being pregnant with Ari, and how much joy I felt.

"Are you excited?"

"About what?"

She looked up from her phone cautiously. Her face was beat to perfection; that much I had to give her. Her skin was glowing. Pregnancy looked good on her.

"The baby. Cedric told us it's a girl."

Her tone changed as she visibly relaxed. She rubbed her stomach and smiled widely. "I'm very excited. I always wanted a little girl. Now, I'm about to have one. She's gonna be spoiled rotten. Between me and Cedric, she ain't gonna be no good."

"She'll probably be a daddy's girl. There's something about men and their daughters. Ari has Jett wrapped around her finger." I instantly regretted my words once they left my mouth. I hadn't intended to bring up my ex-husband at all.

"That's great. Kid's need *both* their parents."

She brushed it off like it wasn't nothing. I realized then, that she had put the situation behind her. I was the one still dwelling on the past.

"You're right. That's one thing I can say. Jett and Ari have a special relationship that's theirs and theirs alone. It gives me time to step out and mingle a bit. Go to weddings and whatnot."

"If it ever starts," Shugg added.

We shared a genuine laugh as I realized Shugg wasn't so bad. Our conversation about kids and life in general continued as we sat there chopping it up like friends. Shugg was funny, down-to-earth, and even gave me a few tips about going braless while still keeping the girls high and covered. I had been engrossed in my own hatred for the girl, that I didn't give her the chance to show me how cool she could be. That was my mistake. Shugg wasn't my enemy. She was caught in a bad situation, that wasn't her fault at all.

"You're alright, Shugg," I told her as I crossed my legs.

"You're not so bad yourself. Once you stop being so mean!"

"Who, me? I don't know what you're talking about."

"Umm hmm, you know...but that's the past."

As if on cue, a waiter up to us with a tray of champagne flutes. I handed one to Shugg and took one for myself. Considering my surroundings, it wasn't the most practical place to have a drink, but at that moment, I really didn't care.

"To new beginnings," I declared, raising my glass.

"To new beginnings," Shugg repeated, before sitting her full glass down on the floor.

NESSA

I needed air. I told myself that this day would be easy, but so far it hadn't been. My nerves were in disarray causing panic within. The subtle feeling started off that morning and festered until coming full circle around the time for the ceremony. I couldn't do it. I couldn't go through with it.

I had every intention on embarrassing Steele just like he embarrassed me. Everyone was getting into place, and I stepped toward the kitchen area to moisten my dry throat. Unfortunately, Steele beat me to it. He snuck off to a quiet area to talk to his side bitch. It just so happened to be in the kitchen, and I got more than an ear full.

"You already know," he stated, as I slowly pushed the swinging doors open. "As soon as this is over, I'm out. I want you in the bed and naked. I'm diving straight in."

He stood with his back toward me, oblivious to my arrival. I inched closer as he continued with his sex talk.

"I'ma fuck the shit outta you, girl. You better be ready." He paused briefly to listen to what she had to say before speaking again. "I can't stay. I'm doing this little honeymoon thing for a few days, but when I get back, I got you. We can do whatever you want."

"Oh really?" I asked, startling him.

My hand caught him mid-turn as I smacked him hard on his face. It stunned him for a minute, causing him to drop his phone. I wasn't done just yet. Filled with adrenaline, I kicked my shoes off and squared up.

"Nessa, what the fuck are you doing?"

What did it look like I was doing? I was about to beat his ass inside of a church. As he stood there, with his guard down, I lunged forward, hitting him in the chest.

"You wanna do me like this on our wedding day?" I screamed, unleashing my fury. My arms flailed wildly, but I managed to get a few licks in.

"Chill out, girl!" he demanded, managing to grab both wrists and hold them down.

I resorted to using my feet. His legs became my target as I kicked until I made contact.

"You're crazy!"

I turned my wrists awkwardly, loosening his grip. I broke free when he tried to reposition his hold. He grabbed for me again, but I pushed his hands away.

"Nessa! Let me explain. Just hear me out."

There was nothing left to say. Our marriage was over. Announcing it to the fifty or so guests in attendance wasn't even worth it anymore. I just wanted to leave and walk away from the source of so much pain in my life.

My eyes landed on the phone that had slipped from his hands. I picked it up and belted it across the room.

"Talk to your bitch!"

I ventured off on foot, escaping through a set of double doors located in the back of the building. I didn't get far before Steele called my name and took off behind me. Running barefoot, I managed to retreat into a wooded area behind the church before Steele caught up with me. His arms locked around my waist, refusing to let me go.

"Get off me!" I struggled to get away, but his grip was vice-like. "Get your fuckin' hands off me!"

"Not until you calm down."

"Why should I? You couldn't even respect me enough to leave your hoes alone for one day! You're pathetic."

"I'm sorry." He spun me around, forcing me to face him. "I was wrong."

"Fuck you and your 'sorry'!"

"You don't mean that. What about us?"

"There is no us! You fucked that up a long time ago. I've been pretending way too long. I won't play second in my own marriage. If you want to be with other women...fine! You can do it without me. This marriage is over."

"I won't happen again. I promise."

"Do you hear yourself? Do you believe the lies coming out of your mouth? It's been happening for years. I know more than you think I do."

He stared at me with confusion in his eyes as he released his grip. The realization that I wasn't playing finally set in.

"What do you know?" he questioned calmly.

"Everything," I mouthed through gritted teeth. "Congratulations, daddy. How many kids does that make now?" I slapped his face just for the hell of it. "You won't give your wife a child, but you'll raw-dog these random hoes like it ain't nothing. Keep doing you. I'm done!"

I stomped back in the direction of the church. I was positive people were questioning where we were, and they deserved to know the truth. They wasted their time.

"Nessa," he pleaded, taking large steps to catch up with me. "I fucked up, okay. What can I do to fix this?"

I stopped dead in my tracks. Was this nigga serious? I spun on my heels and faced him. "Ain't no fixing shit! It's over. Period. End of sentence. You know, you would think that you would have been smarter. I've been a part of this family for a long time, Steele. I've seen things. I know things. The whole family's about to go down. I'm telling everything I know!"

I continued toward the church again. This time, Steele grabbed me with both hands, stopping my departure.

"Look, I know you're mad, but you're talking crazy right now! This is between me and you. Leave everybody else out of it."

"You should have thought about that when you stuck *my* dick in another bitch. You couldn't wait to call Chrysette, could you?" He stared at me with a dumbfounded expression. I couldn't help but to smirk. "Yeah, I know her name. I know everything about the little tramp. I also know what really goes down at Head Bangerz. I know family secrets that would fuck up the St. John clan for good. You've fucked with the wrong one, Steele! You played me for a fool. Now the whole family is gonna watch as I get the last laugh."

"As good as my father has been to you, this is how you're gonna do him? What about Bliss? What has she done to you? My mother? Genesis? Hell, even Emory treats you like fam. This is how you're gonna repay them?"

His words had more meaning than I led on. Steele was the person I wanted to hurt. Everyone else was just collateral damage. He noticed me fumbling with my thoughts and played on my emotions.

"Nessa, I'm sorry. I was wrong. I take full responsibility, but you know how much money the club brings in. Everybody has their own side hustle going on, but in the end, the club is what keeps Uncle Sam and the feds off our back. I can't let you fuck this up for everybody. Tell me what I gotta do. I got my family to think about."

"How ironic? You think about them but didn't give a damn about me."

"That's not true."

"Save it! You want me to keep my mouth shut? Really? Well, you're gonna have to come out of your pocket real nice in order to keep me quiet."

"How much is it gonna take?"

I thought about it for a moment. A set amount wouldn't be sufficient. I wanted money constantly flowing in. It was only right. I deserved it. There was only one way to guarantee that happened.

"I want in."

"What?"

"Like you said...I know how much money the club is bringing in. Your father is stepping down. I want to be a part of it."

"You know that's not gonna happen. My father is dividing Head Bangerz equally. Five kids, ten-percent each."

"That's only fifty-percent."

"The other half belongs to my mother."

I chuckled to myself as Chandra's words rung in my ear, 'you gotta be smart.' She had her husband stepping down from a company *he* started, and she was still the majority owner. I needed to get like her.

"I want *your* portion. That's how much it's gonna cost you."

"Man...you buggin'!"

I shook free from his grip and walked away again. There was no point in wasting time. Steele was going to learn the hard way.

"Nessa!" he called after me. "Nessa!"

I ignored him and continued on my journey. His next words slowed my stride. "Five."

"Ten," I countered.

"Six, and the highest I'm gonna go."

"I'll see you in divorce court."

"Wait, Nessa!" His voice changed an octave as he threw out a higher number. "Seven, that's it."

I stopped but refused to turn around. "Nine."

"Damn, I gotta live too. What about me?"

"What about you?"

"This ain't right." He caught up to me and resumed his negotiation. "Seven point five; and we walk back in there like nothing ever happened."

"That wouldn't have been a good deal...if you hadn't been giving your side bitch *our* money every month. Was the pussy that good?" He knew better than to answer. "Eight point five...and you move out of my house."

"Your house? Shiiiiit...for eight and a half percent, we're sleeping in the same bed and fuckin'!"

"Just because you said that, nine."

"Eight."

"Eight point five. Final offer."

"I'll give you that...on one condition."

I chuckled at his audacity. Raising my hand to my hip, I sucked my teeth loudly. "You're not in any position to be giving demands."

"You're playin' hardball, I get it, but the only way I can guarantee that you ain't gonna fuck me over, is if I keep you close. That means, no divorce. We stay married, live in the same house, and smile for our guests as we recite our vows."

"I got a condition of my own."

"Damn...you're already suckin' me dry. What else could you possibly want?"

"I'll take the eight point five. I'll walk down that aisle, and I might even smile for a picture or two...but if that bitch...let me rephrase that...if *any* bitch pops a baby out of her pussy that belongs to you, all bets are off."

"It's a little too late for that. Chrysette already has a baby."

"And like a dummy, you've been paying for it. That baby ain't yours, but if you want to continue paying for it, that's on you. Spend your one-and-a-half percent however you want. She ain't getting a penny of mine."

"How do you know it ain't mine?"

"Don't ask me any questions. Figure that shit out yourself. Now, do we have a deal or what?"

"But she's already pregnant. How can I agree when I might have a baby on the way? I might already be fucked."

"That's *your* problem. I meant what I said." I turned to walk away again, but he grabbed my arm.

"Why are you doing this?"

"I guess I'm just like you – selfish. Make up your mind. Are we doing this or what?"

He thought long and hard before agreeing to my terms. Together, we walked back toward the church in silence. When we reached the door, he held it open as he muttered, "As fucked up as it may seem, Nessa, I really do love you."

With confidence, I responded, "I love me too."

CONNECT WITH KEISHA ELLE

Facebook 'Like' Page: www.facebook.com/AuthorKeishaElle
Facebook Reading Group:
www.facebook.com/groups/kickinitwithkeisha
Twitter: www.twitter.com/keisha_elle
Instagram: www.instagram.com/keisha_writes
Email: keisha.elle@yahoo.com
Website: www.keishaelle.com

COMING 05/11!

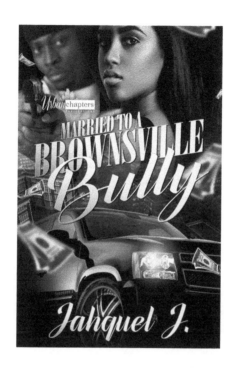

COMING 05/13!

COMING 05/14!

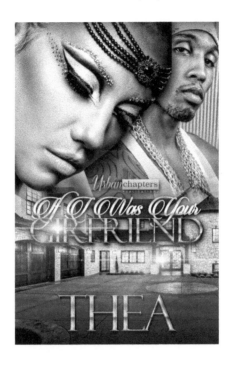

COMING 05/16!

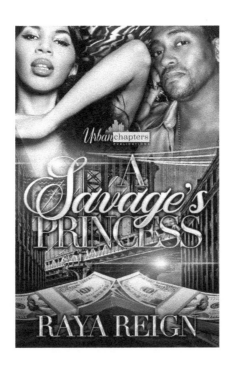

05735276

CPSIA information can be obtained
at www.ICGtesting.com
Printed in the USA
LVHW012147081118
596444LV00017B/397/P

9 781718 993112